T0017248

An Orphan World is extraordinary: an unflinching anatomy of poverty and violence, a harrowingly brave exploration of desire, and also the most beautiful account I've ever read of a son's love for his father. Caputo is a blazing new talent in world literature. Everyone should read this book. **Garth Greenwell**, author of WHAT BELONGS TO YOU

An Orphan World has won Caputo a place on the prestigious Hay Bogota 39 list of the best Latin American writers under 40 years of age. The reasons? This is a powerful, poetic novel that tells a story of rites of passage.
Carlos Pardo, *Babelia* (*El País*)

The novelty of Caputo's prose and the truthfulness of his intuition will leave readers speechless.
Carolina Sanín, author of THE CHILDREN

An Orphan World is a beautiful novel, sad and moving, bold and violent, in which the understanding of the body and of sex is crafted in radical and astonishing ways.
Alia Trabucco Zerán, author of Man Booker International shortlisted THE REMAINDER

An Orphan World blows up conventional forms in order to create something original and delicately beautiful.
Margarita García Robayo, author of FISH SOUP

Caputo has rewritten Colombian violence. (…) This debut novel marks the birth of a great writer.
Laura Restrepo, author of DELIRIUM

An Orphan World is a great novel, profound and complex (…) Readers will feel grateful at the beauty captured by Caputo.
Marianne Ponsford

An Orphan World is a novel both desolate and libertine, a chrysalis in the happening where sometimes the horrific is to the fore (...) I loved its pure poetic essence.
Mageda Baudoin, *El País*

AN ORPHAN WORLD

First published by Charco Press 2019
Charco Press Ltd., Office 59, 44-46 Morningside Road, Edinburgh
EH10 4BF

Copyright © Giuseppe Caputo 2016
Published by arrangement with VicLit Agency
First published in Spanish as *Un mundo huérfano* by
Penguin Random House Group (Colombia)
English translation copyright © Juana Adcock & Sophie Hughes 2019

The rights of Giuseppe Caputo to be identified as the author of this work and of Juana Adcock & Sophie Hughes to be identified as the translators of this work have been asserted by them in accordance with the Copyright, Designs and Patents Act 1988.

All rights reserved. This book is copyright material and must not be copied, reproduced, transferred, distributed, leased, licensed or publicly performed or used in any way except as specifically permitted in writing by the publisher, as allowed under the terms and conditions under which it was purchased or as strictly permitted by the applicable copyright law. Any unauthorised distribution or use of this text may be a direct infringement of the author's and publisher's rights, and those responsible may be liable in law accordingly.

A CIP catalogue record for this book is available from the British Library.

ISBN: 978-1-9164656-2-6
e-book: 978-1-9164656-9-5

www.charcopress.com

Edited by Annie McDermott & Fionn Petch
Cover design by Pablo Font
Typeset by Laura Jones
Proofread by Fiona Mackintosh

This book was selected to receive financial assistance from English PEN's 'PEN Translates' programme, supported by Arts Council England. English PEN exists to promote literature and our understanding of it, to uphold writers' freedoms around the world, to campaign against the persecution and imprisonment of writers for stating their views, and to promote the cooperation of writers and the free exchange of ideas.
www.englishpen.org

Giuseppe Caputo

AN ORPHAN WORLD

Translated by
Juana Adcock & Sophie Hughes

CHARCO PRESS

A butterfly fluttered down to a dark place;
of beautiful colours it seemed;
it was hard to tell.

Marosa Di Giorgio

CHAPTER I

The Cardboard Star

We're cloaked in black light tonight. That's why the men can't see each other. At most they see violet teeth, which disappear for moments in the violet smoke, or in encounters with other teeth. Then the moon, a ball glowing purple in the light, purple like their teeth, comes into view. And as it appears, white shafts of light rise from the floor, intermittently setting bodies and faces aglow. And that's why the men, fragmented in the light, scintillating in the rays, look like stars. They quiver and flicker, those stars, and the newfound brightness to the place is the brightness of the full moonlit sky.

The men hug and holler. They crowd together, delirious, jostling to get closer to the sphere. They raise their arms as if trying to touch it.

'You too,' one of them says to me. 'Come in closer!' I do as he says, letting him lead me astray. I thread my way through until I'm directly beneath the ball, which starts to descend: the moon starts to descend.

The beams of light turn green, and with them, the faces. Then the music changes: louder now, now slower. The music is dripping. The men change too: they all switch off for a beat. They gaze at the moon from behind the smoky haze, and there they remain, gazing. But they are in total darkness again, and even the moon disappears, only to reappear bigger, whiter, closer.

Now the mirrors on the ball are visible: I see us in its facets. The men come back to life and start dancing again. In among them, I feel something brimming: time, bubbling, spilling out of me; space, like me, giving way. And still the moon descends. The men go on dancing. One of them, whirling around in circles, stops, disoriented.

'What's with all the clothes? Aren't you hot?' he asks, caressing me.

He takes off my shirt, smells it, and starts waving it in the air. Then he spots my star, plastered to my sweaty chest. He looks at it, looks at me. And, just like that, the time rewinds…

* * *

One night, many nights ago, my dad gave me a star. We lived in the red, as we do now, in a sad house with next to no furniture. And since the house was sad, and its white walls were bare, my dad decided to decorate. Taking inspiration from cave paintings, so primally ancient, more ancient than this story by thousands of years, he began his artistic project by drawing a crayon cow on the kitchen wall: two black circles, one on top of the other, and two triangles for the ears. He added a tail, coiled like a spring, and for a face two dots – the eyes – and a smiling curve.

'All that's missing is the nose,' my dad said, and he drew a nose: two dots, like the eyes, only bigger. Once he'd finished, he pointed at the sketch and said, pensively, 'Cow'.

Then he went to my room where, as if gauging what he needed for his next creation, he stood contemplating the ceiling. He tried to touch it, clambering onto the bed, but he still couldn't reach. He asked me to bring him a chair. His idea was to put the chair on the bed and then climb on top of it. I told him to forget it.

'You could fall, Pa. You could split your head open, break your hip. Come on, the chair might break. We don't have furniture to go around breaking.'

Clearly annoyed, he turned his back on me and began drawing on the wall next to the door: a circle, again, and some lines for a torso, arms and legs. Above the stick man he wrote, 'Pa'.

'Love you, son,' he said.

With our arms around each other we went to his room, and there he drew another tiny body in the exact spot where the light shone – the light that was never turned out, since Pa was scared of being plunged into total darkness. And with the black crayon he drew a heart around the little man.

'You, my darling,' he said, and kissed me on the forehead. I sensed it was time to say something, show him some affection, even support his creative venture, so I stared at the portrait in silence, mimicking the way he'd stared at the ceiling.

'You know,' I said finally, 'it makes me want to tear out this piece of wall, frame it, and hang it right back up again, like a painting.'

My dad listened, perplexed but gratified, and carried on drawing.

We lived in a neighbourhood with no street lights. It was dark, at night I mean, even though it was at the bottom of Lights Avenue. Three immensities surrounded us there: the city on one side, an electric forest; the sea on the other, made to seem darker against the bright city; and the sky above, the same as always, constantly erupting, sometimes into rain, sometimes into thunder, or into stars, into moon.

Lights Avenue cut right through the city. That's where the parks were, all lit up, and the huge houses like castles. They called it Lights Avenue because of all the street lights, which were packed together at the start, still plentiful in the middle stretch, and then dotted infrequently towards the end, gradually petering out as the street approached our neighbourhood. One by one the lamps went out, or simply hung back, as if avoiding the edge, or as if the street itself grew gloomier the closer it came to where we lived. But nearby was the sea, eternal; the old, spent sea, and sometimes it left on the sand the most unlikely offerings.

One night, as my dad and I strolled along the beach, we noticed the waves had washed a sofa onto the shore. And that sofa – bright red, run aground – was covered in seaweed.

'If it's not rotten,' Pa said, 'we'll take it home. We could do with a sofa.'

I moved in closer to inspect it and the stench knocked me for six. I cried out and retched.

'That bad, eh?' he teased.

'Nah, not too bad at all,' I replied.

Once I'd recomposed myself, I grabbed a handful of seaweed, slapped it on my head and jumped up and down saying, 'Look at my hair, so lush and long!' I danced and strutted about. Pa laughed, we both laughed, and we carried on along the shore.

The sea's detritus was so baffling it was beautiful: clocks washed up on the sand, many still working, the minute and second hands marking the exact time. And alongside the clocks there'd be driftwood – coconut branches or broomsticks, which Pa would use to sweep up the foam, sending it back to the water. The sea also carried lamps on its waves, and since they were never on, each time my dad came across one he'd say, 'Let's hope one of these nights the light holds out.' And with that, we'd slowly make our way home, arm in arm, pondering the causes and quandaries of our poverty.

'We're broke,' my dad said, the night he gave me the star. He chuckled as he said it, as if accepting his lot, our lot, and I looked at him, worried, and tired, too, of worrying, and annoyed at him for having laughed. As I sat thinking what to do, how to keep the house afloat, how to keep us afloat, Pa picked up a square piece of cardboard from the floor. He cut around the corners, transforming it into a star. Then he poked a tiny hole in it and threaded a length of wool through the hole. Finally, he tied the ends and hung the new chain around my neck.

'To remind you, my shining light, that we still have love.'

★ ★ ★

And precisely because the light is black tonight, all white things, as I was saying, look violet: the men's teeth, but also the whites of their eyes. When they kiss and wet the lips of one man, of another, their teeth, glowing violet, disappear. And since they close their eyes as their lips meet, their violet eyeballs vanish too. Those kisses make the darkness darker.

All the while, the moon keeps descending. The closer it gets to the stage, the louder they shout, the more they dance. Out of nowhere, another light stops them in their tracks – no, it stills them: the men go on dancing, but as if in slow motion, their frenzied movements stilled for a second, stilled again the next, slow. Each man looks like two men, like one, like several.

Eventually, the moon ends its descent. It shines bright, and, stationed at the centre, between the jumping crowd and the domed ceiling, it begins to open: like an egg it begins to crack, and the men, dazzled, stop dancing or looking at one another. They stare instead at the moon, and they applaud it, glistening in all that light and sweat, beaming in the light of the moon, which finally opens out like a seashell.

'Good evening!' booms a voice, and giddily we reply, 'Good evening!'

Only Luna exists, emerging beautiful, handsome, from the moon. All lit up, she (he) waves down at us. All lit up, he (she) poses, singing, '*No, I'll never fall in love again… I gave you my hands: you shattered them. And my feet, oh, my feet: you walked all over them. How can I run to you with this pain in my step aching right down to my soul? How can I slap your face, sweet fool, with this pair of broken hands?*'

Someone beside me speaks, anticipating the string of ballads we'll be subjected to for the rest of the night.

'Oh, this is bad… he's on the rebound.'

Luna pulls away from the microphone and starts to drink, gulping from the bottle, forgetting we're there. Some boo. We all stop watching her.

'Arseholes,' Luna says suddenly. 'Pay attention.' And she starts crooning again.

I look around for the guy who stole my shirt and spot him grinding against a pillar, arms in the air. He smiles, convinced I'm giving him the eye, and blows me a kiss. So I walk over, feigning indifference, and tell him I just want my shirt back. Laughing to himself, the man shows me his empty hands.

'If you've lost it,' I say, 'you'll have to give me yours. I don't care how sweaty it is.'

I stare at him blankly, then expectantly, waiting for some kind of reaction, but the man just gives me the finger and rubs himself up and down against the pillar, looking ridiculous. I turn away, and just as I'm thinking, in a rage, that I don't have shirts to go around losing, I feel a tap on my shoulder.

'Spoilsport,' he says, 'killjoy, tight-arse. You can stay alone then, with your manky little star.'

The moment he's facing the other way I toss an ice cube at him vindictively, but it hits someone else on the head. And this guy seems baffled at first, but quickly turns aggressive.

'What's your problem?'

'Finally, you notice me!' I improvise on the spot before planting a kiss on him.

* * *

From the outside, our house looked like a head of wild hair, its roof tiles all out of place. Inside, it was like a building site: lots of the floor tiles – black and white like a chequerboard – had come loose, and wobbled when we stepped on them. You could see pipes and cables poking out here and there.

Our living room had one big window, which looked out onto the street. We never put up curtains; there was no money for that.

'Why would we cover the view with curtains,' my dad said, 'when we've got a wall-to-wall work of art right here?'

And Pa would sit, sometimes for hours on end, staring out onto the street in a state of perpetual wonder, giving titles to each of the paintings as they formed before his eyes, 'Still Life with Bins', 'The Star Belt', 'Birds on a Power Cable', 'Thief with Victim', 'Roadkill Cat', 'Lone Man Picking Up Cigarette', 'Lovers in the Night', 'Moonless Sky', 'Self-Portrait in Silence', 'Nocturnal Nude'.

Whenever I walked into the room and he spotted my reflection in the window, my dad would say, 'The Apparition of the Son'.

I, too, would gaze out of the window sometimes, and neighbours and passers-by would look back at me. Having noticed the bare living room, scantily furnished with a couple of chairs, they would rap at the window and ask if the house was for sale.

'Piss off,' I'd tell them. 'Leave us alone.'

Musicians would pass by too, on their way to the bar district or back, and on seeing the house they'd laugh.

'Well, well, a window made for serenading,' they'd mock us, before striking up a tune and loitering until I had to pee on them to make them leave.

Then, one night, as he gazed out of the window, Pa had one of his epiphanies. 'I've got it! I've had an idea. Come on. We're off to the bar to make some money.'

I said that if we went to the bar we'd only end up *spending* money, and that I was done with buying on credit.

'Don't be such a sourpuss, come on.'

I reminded him that fewer and fewer people hung out at The Letcher now, that it would just be the same old guys with the same old gals, each more broke than the last, to which Pa, clearly tired of listening to me, responded, voice raised, with his favourite line:

'Don't answer back.'

So I kept my dismay and despair to myself as we left the house, and, once we were outside, Pa explained that there were a lot of sad men in the bar in need of advice.

'And where's the money in that?' I asked, genuinely intrigued, and anticipating, besides, a bad night.

'It couldn't be simpler: I'll offer advice to whoever wants it. The first piece is free, and from then on I charge. Winos generally value my experience.'

This made me laugh and also decide that, even though it was a terrible plan, a change of scene would do me good. We put our arms on each other's shoulders and walked like that all the way to The Letcher. When we arrived, there was a new bouncer on the door.

'Come on in, congratulations!' he said, and he tossed a handful of tiny paper hearts into the air. I gawped at him, my eyes two question marks.

'It's Couples Night,' the man explained.

'Excuse me,' my dad elbowed past impatiently, perhaps feeling uncomfortable. Stepping inside, we spotted two couples. The first pair weren't even looking at each other as they sipped their drinks. The second were having an argument. At the bar, as if they hadn't moved since the last time we saw them, were Ramón-Ramona – serving – and The Three Toupées: Alirio, Simón and Chickpeas. We called them that, Toupées, because all three of them, despite showing clear signs of balding, modelled haircuts ranging from wacky to desperate. It was hard to tell if they were trying to emphasise their baldness or mask it as far as humanly possible. Ramón-Ramona was sporting the same look as ever: a hat, trousers and a waistcoat embroidered in different colours. There was also the fake beauty spot drawn just above the mouth.

My dad went over and greeted the fighting couple, pulling up a stool as if he'd been invited.

'Talk it out, that's the way,' he said. They both stared at him, but before either could get a word in he added, this time just for the lady, 'It's good to hear him out, but you don't have to be his dustbin. You don't have to take his rubbish. Don't ever become an emotional dumping ground.'

I rolled my eyes, turned away from the unfolding scene, and sat down at the bar between Simón and Chickpeas. Ramón-Ramona put a glass of water down in front of me and told me, in a friendly but firm tone, that we couldn't keep adding our drinks to the tab. I said no problem, thanks, I understood, and Ramón-Ramona replied with a wink, 'But you know you two are always welcome.'

I mentioned the bouncer throwing heart-shaped confetti at my dad and me.

'Here's to my favourite couple!' Ramón-Ramona chuckled.

'Anyway, what happened to the other guy on the door?' I asked.

'Oh, nothing, kid. He got knifed.'

My dad was back.

'Nothing?' he said. 'You call that nothing? Imagine how deserted that poor doorman would feel if he could hear you, Ramón-Ramona. Take my advice: look out for the people around you. It's important to know how to look out for yourself, to practise self-care and all that, but others deserve the same treatment. You think it over.'

'I was just telling your son here that I can't give you any more drinks on credit,' Ramón-Ramona replied drily, wiping down the bar. 'I'll get you a glass of water.'

'And another tip,' Pa went on. 'A little exercise I'd recommend: buy yourself an egg and treat it as you would a child. Draw on it, if you like: a little face. Put it in a basket, wrap it up in some serviettes, and take it everywhere you go. The challenge is not to drop it.'

'And why would I go around carrying an egg when I could just eat it?' Ramón-Ramona laughed again. 'With the way this food shortage is going...'

'To learn how to care for others, that's why. And I'm afraid I'm going to have to charge you: the first piece of advice is free, and after that it's a hundred a pop.'

'Well I'm afraid *I'm* going to have to get out my little red book,' Ramón-Ramona replied with raised eyebrows. 'You two are on every page.'

'And Chickpeas is probably in there too,' Simón said.

'Chickpeas less.'

'Well, he'll soon catch up,' Alirio chipped in. 'With all that pent-up rage. He's already downed three-quarters of the bottle.'

'What's up with you?' I asked Chickpeas.

'Tell me all about it,' Pa said. 'The first piece of advice is free, the second will set you back a round hundred.'

'I thought my neighbour was dead,' Chickpeas began, 'but it turns out he's alive and kicking, and he's eaten my dog Paws.'

'That's awful,' Simón said.

'No, no, no,' interrupted Ramón-Ramona, 'Tell us properly, from the start. What happened?'

'We're dealing with two separate issues here,' my dad recapped. 'Death, and the dog.'

'I hadn't seen my neighbour for weeks,' Chickpeas went on. 'We'd always wave hello, you know, window to window, whenever we turned on the light. Then, one night, I just stopped seeing him.'

'Very important, that, cordiality among neighbours,' my dad remarked. 'And respect, too, of course. But you don't have to respect everyone. Not everyone deserves respect.'

'Yeah, cheers for that!' the man from the fighting couple shouted over to the bar. 'I owe you a hundred, you old git!'

'You don't need to put up with him!' my dad called back, but to the woman. 'Forget about him! There's no shame in being on your own.'

The man went on yelling. The woman, meanwhile, had begun hitting him.

'Are you scaring off my clients?' Ramón-Ramona said. 'I'm watching you.'

The couple stormed out of the bar and I caught sight of the bouncer tossing hearts over them as they passed. Chickpeas took another swig and went on with his story.

'The nights went by and I still hadn't seen hide nor hair of my neighbour. I snuck looks through his window when I took Paws out, and the table was always laid but there was never any food on it. Just a glass, a plate, and a knife and fork. Not so much as a slice of bread.'

'It's not sounding good,' I said, merely to contribute something to the conversation.

'My neighbour thought Paws was — ach! — *well fed*. "You've fattened him up!" he shouted from his window one night when I took Paws out for his walk. But it was just his fur, it made him look chubby.'

'Nothing wrong with loving your pet,' Alirio said, and Pa shot him a furious look, as if Alirio were muscling in on his moneymaking scheme.

'Paws would sometimes escape out the door,' Chickpeas went on. 'But he'd always come back after a while like a good boy. As if he missed me. And I'd be waiting for him in the living room, and we'd play fetch.'

'Beautiful,' Simón said, and I noticed that Ramón-Ramona was snickering, eyes fixed on the sink, mouth zipped.

'I haven't seen my baby since last night. A few hours ago, on my way here, I looked in through my neighbour's window, and there the guy was, after all those nights of *not* being there — leaning back in his chair, rubbing his belly with the look of a man who's had his fill of dog.'

'Not good,' Alirio said. 'Not much to be done there.'

'A word of advice,' Pa cut in. 'You need some flowers in the house.'

'What for?' Chickpeas asked.

'To lift your spirits.'

'OK, OK, time out,' Ramón-Ramona said, eyes brimming with tears from holding in the laughter for so long. 'I very much doubt the neighbour's eaten Paws. I'm sure the little mutt will show up.'

'I'm not so sure,' Chickpeas said, and he burst into tears with the bottle clutched to his chest.

My dad took a deep breath but, just as he was about to offer another piece of advice, Ramón-Ramona pointed at our glasses, then at the drinks display.

'What'll it be? They're on the house!'

We all clapped and broke into song, and at that moment a drunk stumbled up to the bar.

'I look at you and I'm all confused. What exactly are you?' he asked.

'Can't you tell?' Ramón-Ramona asked in return.

'I can't, no. That's why I asked. Are you a man or a woman?' the man went on.

'Come here and I'll show you,' Ramón-Ramona said. A second later, having got a flash of the underside of Ramón-Ramona's apron, the drunk took off with his head hanging down.

That night we all left the bar well oiled. As we said our goodbyes, the bouncer sprinkled us with more little hearts. My dad and I went to the beach, but the waves had only washed up pebbles and shells. The sofa was still there, beached; not so red now, and the air around it still unfit for breathing. Exhausted, Pa sat down on it.

'I promise you, son.' he said. 'We're going to get out of this fix.'

I told him not to think about it any more, not to worry, that I was going to provide for us both.

'We'll think of something, Pa.'

Later, the waves – silent, moribund, spread smooth like blankets – brought the naked bodies of three old men back to the shore.

'Or maybe they were young,' I thought, 'but they'd been in the water a long time.'

* * *

'Get *off*,' I tell the man kissing me. He pulls away, but there's a determined look on his face. He tries to gauge whether I've really had enough, and then he kisses me again. I grab hold of his cock, pretending to reciprocate the kiss.

'You see?' he says. 'See how badly you want me?'

And I keep pursing my fingers around him, tighter now, emotionless, and then tighter and tighter until he lets out a groan and walks off.

Meanwhile, Luna, sitting on the ball, starts lobbing ice cubes at us.

'The worst crowd I've had in years,' she complains, looking deeply insulted. 'What do you think I am – a piñata?'

And she begins a new song, '*Dead inside, oh, my dearest fool.*' The men laugh and throw polystyrene cups at her. As they rain down, I pick them off the floor to throw back at them.

'Arseholes!' I shout at two of the men. And, louder, 'Louts!'

Tired of looking for my shirt, I decide to leave. Pushing away arms and lips, I make my way towards the door.

'What's eating you?' a man asks. 'Stay.'

I look back before leaving: Luna is up there, climbing up and up; just her astride a moon, the moon that descended and cracked open like an egg. And now she rises higher, where fewer and fewer cups can reach her. 'There's no shame, Luna, in being on your own,' I said to myself.

Outside it looks like there are two nights: one black, the other black and blue. A man points at my bare chest.

'What went on in there, then?' he asks.

I ignore him, but he hurries after me.

'You obviously don't waste any time,' he says, lustful, but also bitter, snubbed.

'How much for the necklace?' another man jokes, and he pulls out a coin. 'Come here, I'll buy it off you.'

I inhale a mouthful of thick, filthy air and walk along an imaginary straight line down the middle of the pavement. Two more men are chatting, sitting on the kerb. They must be about my age. They smile, I smile. One of them opens his mouth to speak, but I motion goodbye with a wave of my hand and carry on along my invisible line. They stay behind.

I slip softly into the house, leaving my shoes outside so as not to wake my dad. But he's still up. Night after night he's been like this.

'The Apparition of the Son,' he says with his eyes fixed on the window.

I give him a hug and a kiss. And he looks at my star.

'It's lasted well, that cardboard,' he says.

I undress down to my underpants and we go to bed.

'Did you have fun?' he asks.

'Yeah. I missed you.'

'You've got to make the most of it, son. You don't get these years back.'

We lie in silence, staring up at the ceiling. Several minutes of silence later, and just as he did on the night he gave me the star, my dad says, 'We're broke'. He glances at me worriedly; tired, too, of worrying. Just like I was, on the night he called me 'my shining light', reminding us that we still have love.

CHAPTER II

The Talking House

That's how we lived, my dad and I, in that grey neighbourhood – a grey that was sometimes smoky, sometimes blackish – trapped in a cycle of poverty and never quite at peace. Each time the kitchen cupboards began to look bare (we ate eggs more than anything else), each time the banknotes became coins and the coins fewer coins, each time we had to pawn a piece of furniture, an item of clothing, some appliance or other, my dad would lose sleep and gaze at the ceiling for nights on end until he came up with a plan to buy back our things, turn the coins into banknotes and restock the cupboards.

At one point he wanted to become a tailor, but it became clear, when he attempted to mend his own clothes, that he could barely sew a hem.

'Practice makes perfect,' I said. 'These things take time.'

And while he did make a go of it, my dad soon ran out of patience.

'Not my thing,' he said, settling the matter.

His next great plan was to sell pies, which we would make together. But people started turning up at the house without any money and he never had the heart to charge them, or he simply didn't know how to.

'Eat up, eat up. Pay me later,' he'd say, ever industrious, from the window where he served them. The pie business went bust before it had even formally opened. Pa eventually figured that perhaps the neighbours had been taking advantage.

'Some of them had the money and they just played dumb,' he said one night.

And so the cycle of poverty would start all over again: he'd stare at the food cupboard, stop sleeping, come up with an idea, try to pull it off, fail, stare at the food cupboard, stop sleeping, come up with an idea, try to pull it off, fail... Between one failure and the next we would either take out credit or pawn something, until the money ran out again and the time came to find some more.

One night, my dad called to me from the kitchen, where he was frying an egg.

'See that?' he said. 'Tell me you see it.'

'Yeah,' I said. 'You told me it was egg for dinner.'

He rolled his eyes and gave me a ticking off: all I ever thought about was food. Pa hadn't slept for several nights and the lack of sleep was making him increasingly tetchy. I decided it was better not to argue.

He told me the egg looked like a lion, and that the sound of the stove made it look like it was roaring.

'You take over dinner,' he said. 'I've had an idea.'

He turned around and with a crayon began to draw more of his sketches on the wall: a circle with arrows – a clock, perhaps – and some kind of window or door. Above all that he wrote, 'Blah, blah, blah'.

Next he drew a mirror and, beside that, a frying pan. Above them, too, he wrote, 'Blah, blah, blah'. I pressed the egg with the back of the spoon: yellow oozed across the white and I told Pa dinner was nearly ready.

'It'll be done in two secs. Just waiting for the yolk to cook through.'

'But I like it runny!' he shouted from the living room.

'No, no. It's easier to cut if it's cooked through.'

'I like it runny,' Pa repeated, pretending he hadn't heard me.

I cut our egg in two – cooked through, in the end – and gave the bigger portion to my dad, who was gazing at his drawings, deep in thought.

'It's harder to share when it's runny,' I said.

'That's alright. Mm, delicious,' Pa replied, still focused on his drawings.

On the wall he had drawn some swirls like waves churning around a giant sofa. I guessed it was the sea, our sea, carrying the sofa to the shore. I couldn't always make sense of my dad's scrawls, but that night he drew a triangle on top of a square and straight away I recognised it as a house. He added the door, the windows, and finally, once again, the words 'Blah, blah, blah'.

'What I'm thinking,' Pa said, 'is to turn this house into an attraction and open it up to the public. That'll be a nice little earner.'

'What do you mean, an attraction?' I asked as I ate my half of the egg.

'We'll call it The Talking House,' he said, almost thinking aloud. 'It'll be the neighbourhood's first ever landmark: the house that talks, welcomes the locals and tells them what it's feeling.'

I lost interest in the idea even as I listened. My instinct told me it wouldn't work, and that not only would it not earn us a penny, but we'd probably end up even worse off. My dad carried on talking, though, muttering something about tape recorders and different voices. He said we didn't need much and that we could ask at the second-hand store if they'd lend us a cassette player.

'And if they insist on charging us for it,' he said, 'we'll pay them with the money we got for your bed. Or, better still, with what they pay us.'

'With what *who* pays us?' I asked, knowing full well that my dad would now launch into a bit of optimistic accounting.

'Our punters! Who else? They'll be lining up to pay for entry to The Talking House.'

'Paying to see what exactly?'

'What kind of a question...' he tutted, before making a start on his egg. 'Wouldn't you pay for a conversation with all this, with your house? Wouldn't you pay to know what it thinks, what all the objects in it are feeling – the furniture, the stove? By my calculations, we'll be hiring staff in a matter of weeks.'

'This is worse than I thought,' I said to myself, laughing and crying inside. Still, I couldn't help but find my dad's ideas endearing. He'd moved on to talking about the conversations that the objects might have with each other, that the house might have with the objects, or the objects with the visitors and the visitors with the house.

'I'm thinking that the chair,' he said, 'could ask guests to sit down on it. Insistently at first, then flirtatiously, like it was really up for having a nice pair of buttocks on its lap.'

I burst out laughing. My dad laughed too.

'I don't know whether you're being soft or you've completely lost the plot,' I told him, 'but let's give it a go. All hands on deck! We'd better get the house ready.'

And together we began planning how to bring the few items we owned to life – how to give them a voice.

* * *

How many nights ago did we open The Talking House? Two, it dawns on me. Just two. And yet it still feels as though that night hasn't ended. It's still going on: that night, this night. I try to think about it as being in the past. In the distant past, so as to drive it far away from me. But on it goes. I can hear the voices – 'Horrible, horrible,' and, 'Oh, God. Oh, God.' I'm still leaving the house, walking among the bodies. That's it: the bodies. I can still see them.

And how long has Pa been gone? I wait for him outside the house, curled up into myself as I fiddle with my star, sniffing the cardboard, sucking on the woollen chain.

'Don't go out. It's dangerous. You could get yourself killed,' he told me.

A bus goes by, heaving with people and seemingly about to break down. There are boxes and suitcases on the roof (some of them, looking worse for wear, are about to topple off), and inside I can see people sitting, people standing, even people perched on top of each other. I also think I spot what used to be my bed, caster wheels and all: it's tied with thick ropes to the back of the bus as if it were a trailer, with some stuff in bin bags and a teddy bear on top.

I look at the bed and then at the sky: it saddens me that it doesn't look boundless, that it's not brimming with light. All that fire gone unseen...

'The other night,' a man says, catching me unawares, 'I saw you in the club.'

I smile, but I don't recognise him.

'What's a guy like you doing all on his own?' the man asks me.

I smile again, then glance up the road to the corner in search of my dad: he's not there. I look the other way: he's not there either.

'I'm moving out of the neighbourhood,' he explains, and I notice he's made a makeshift backpack from a bed sheet. 'Don't you want to say goodbye? This is rock hard.'

'Sorry, I'm waiting for someone.'

'We won't be long. At least give me a little kiss.'

'No.'

'Please.'

'No.'

'Well, fuck you, then.'

The man walks away.

'Best of luck!' I call after him, but he doesn't reply or even look round. A line of cars is now backed up behind the bus and my old bed. They are packed together so closely they look like train carriages. Their headlights act as street lights in the night. Light, at long last, down this end of the street – the street that grows brighter and brighter the further it gets from our neighbourhood, as if it were glad to leave us behind.

Finally, my dad appears carrying a box. He's cradling it in his arms like a baby.

'What took you so long? I was worried,' I say, giving him a kiss.

'Surprise!'

He pulls out a loaf of bread and points in the direction of the cars.

'It's still warm. I left it on a running engine for a good long while.'

He looks wide-eyed with bewilderment, only his eyes are no wider open than usual. I realise, for the first time, that his eyes are always like that: in perpetual shock; on constant alert, as if witnessing true horror.

And the bus, the cars, they remain gridlocked…

'Everyone's leaving,' I say, instead of what I really want to say, which is, 'Shall we go too? What do we do now?'

'They'll be back. You'll see,' he says, and someone hoots their horn. 'We're staying put.'

That car horn is followed by another, and then a few more. And the din, like the darkness before it, becomes its own landscape.

★ ★ ★

A few nights before we opened The Talking House, my dad decided we should do an inventory of our belongings. As if it were essential to count them. As if there were even the slightest chance of things going missing in our bare home.

'Write this down,' he said, bossily.

I took the crayon and a piece of card.

'One crayon, and one piece of card,' I wrote.

My dad kept a close eye on proceedings.

'Very good, but you need to be more specific. Write down the colour of the crayon.'

So, next to 'crayon' I wrote 'black' before taking his dictation.

'One mirror, oval, no frame. Gift from the ocean.'

'That's really long,' I said. 'I'm just going to write "mirror".'

'No, sir. And you can add: "Comes with hard-wearing wire for hanging".'

'Fine. What else? The clock…'

'One wall clock, no alarm, shaped like a house. Red hands with animals at the tips: an owl, a fish and a kitty.'

'There isn't room for all of that.'

'Write smaller, then.'

'I can't, the crayon's too fat.'

'Of course you can. What do you mean you can't?'

And we went on like that for a good while longer, until the inventory was complete with the fan, my dad's bed (and its corresponding mattress), the tape recorder and a cassette (which my dad had bought with some of the money he got for my bed), the frying pan, the table, two glasses and two chairs. Everything else had either been sold or pawned, or we'd never owned it.

'Ah, we've missed something,' Pa said.

'What's that?'

'The soap. Write: "Detergent powder for coloured clothes. Also useful for personal hygiene and cleaning dishes".'

'Causes itching and rashes,' I added.

★ ★ ★

I scratch my chest as I peer out of the window. The cars and buses continue to file by. They're all heading for the city. Every now and then my dad and I spot a horse: bolting down the road, out of control (usually followed by a man, careering after it), or pulling carts and cars loaded with boxes, suitcases and people. There is also a lot of horn hooting. On my way to the kitchen I hear my dad say, 'Still Life with Animals and Tyres.' From the hallway I see a man outside walking towards us, waving his arms.

'What's he saying?' Pa asks. 'I can't understand him.'

He opens the window and I head back into the living room to stand at his side.

'Can you tell me where the bar district is?' the man asks.

'Everyone else is leaving and you're only just arriving,' I say.

'Are they still there? The bodies, I want to see them.'

'They're still there, yeah. Follow this road straight all the way down,' I say to him.

'And watch out for the horses,' Pa adds.

'Thanks, thanks.'

I go back to the kitchen once the man has gone.

★ ★ ★

And so, to advertise the grand opening of our house of

wonders, we wrote on a piece of cardboard, 'Coming soon to your neighbourhood – exciting new attraction!' We placed the sign in the living room window and rehearsed – as if there were already visitors at the door – the operation that would give life and a voice to the house and all the objects in it. Essentially, the idea consisted of playing a tape that my dad had pre-recorded, putting on the voices for every object, nook and cranny in the house. The trick was to conceal the tape recorder in one of our pockets (preferably the back trouser pocket) and to sync up every action on the tape with the tour of the space we'd give our visitors. So, for example, at the entrance we would hear the door – or rather, my dad's voice on the tape – welcoming everyone to the house. And on passing the living room we would hear the chairs talking.

'Timing,' my dad said, 'is everything. Remember that.'

'Yeah, yeah.'

But come opening night, there was nobody outside queuing to get in when we opened our doors to the public. We headed to The Letcher to recruit our first punters.

'We're bound to pick up one or two there,' Pa said.

And yet, on arriving we noticed there was no bouncer (neither the one who'd been stabbed nor the heart-sprinkler). The only people inside were The Three Toupées.

'Where's Ramón-Ramona?' I asked.

'Bathroom,' Chickpeas said. 'Shouldn't be long.'

'So how are you?'

'Down,' he said, taking a sip of his drink. 'Really down about my neighbour.'

'What's he done now?'

'Oh, the usual, mate. Munching his way through the dogs on the block. One by one, he won't stop till he's eaten them all.'

'Don't start this again,' said Ramón-Ramona, now

back behind the bar. 'I'm beginning to think you're the one eating all the dogs.'

'How dare you?' Chickpeas said.

'Oh, Jesus,' Alirio said, 'I've been thinking the same.'

'I'll eat you if you're not careful.'

'Watch it, fellas,' Simón chipped in. 'He's more than capable.'

'I'd have no qualms about it.'

Meanwhile, my dad was scanning the bar. I suppose he was looking at how empty it was, letting the sorry state of the neighbourhood sink in, as if the space were forcing him to grasp just how bad it had got. I watched him and wondered how seriously those empty tables would affect him, how much sleep he'd lose as a result. And I wondered how he was going to react: whether he'd be distressed or paralysed or carry on as usual. I fretted about what we were going to do, what we could do.

'I've been thinking,' Ramón-Ramona said, 'that it'd be good to give the bar a new name. You know, a bit of novelty, to draw the customers back.'

'What have you got in mind?' Simón asked.

'The Catfight,' he said. 'Or Stomach Pump.'

'I prefer The Letcher.'

'But the new name would be written in neon letters…'

My dad chuckled as he listened to them, and, clearly encouraged by the conversation, he invited them over to the house.

'There have been some strange goings on,' he said, trying to wink at me on the sly, but failing hopelessly. 'Voices.'

'Now, that is serious,' Alirio said. 'Ghosts are no laughing matter.'

'They're not ghosts,' I explained, and my dad elbowed me.

'Let him think what he likes,' he hissed. 'That way the

surprise will be even better.'

'The only voice I can hear is Paws,' Chickpeas sighed. 'Poor dog must have yowled his heart out. He must have suffered so much.'

As Ramón-Ramona locked up for the night we noticed a group of men queuing to go into Luna, the club over the road.

'They're the only ones who come round these parts nowadays,' someone said, perhaps Simón.

My dad stood staring at the crowd. I could see he was thinking it was his chance to secure some takers for The Talking House. But those men were only there to have a dance and see Luna perform. I doubted they'd want to come with us. I doubted even more that they'd pay a penny to enter our house and listen to those tape recordings.

My dad was still staring so in order to stop things from turning ugly, I proposed that we take Ramón-Ramona to see the house first, as a kind of repayment for all the drinks that had gone on the tab.

'That's a decent number with The Three Toupées on board too. We can come back another time to recruit more visitors,' I said.

'Alright,' he replied, but without looking at me.

Given that he usually got the hump when I disagreed with him, I was surprised by how easy he was to convince.

'You OK?' I asked.

'Yes, yes.'

'Sure?'

'Yes.'

We walked together to the house, gazing at the electric forest in the distance. I liked to contemplate it almost without blinking: now and then I'd spot when someone turned on a light, and when they did, it looked like the forest was growing before my eyes. Then that light, or a different one, would go out, and this happened over and again until the forest changed shape, for a moment, changed height, for a moment, lit up the night, the forest buried in night, starry, for a moment, the forest twinkling, sparkling electric, luminous, for a moment, for a moment, for a moment.

* * *

I drop an egg into the water, which is already boiling. I watch both the egg and the water with an ache in the pit of my stomach (the car horns in the background, the car horns), and a sense of foreboding: as if the sea, from now on, would no longer bring us gifts but horrors; as if the waves would reach all the way to the house and take back the objects it once gave us, before taking us too.

'Don't tell me you're leaving as well,' I hear my dad shout. 'This really is sad news.'

'I'm battening down the hatches,' Ramón-Ramona says from outside the window. 'But I can't say I'm not tempted.'

'We're staying too,' I say.

'The Toupées are off, by the looks of things,' my dad adds. 'Chickpeas has already left.'

'Do me a favour, will you?' Ramón-Ramona interrupts. 'Look after this computer for a while. Use it, if you like. I'm trying to sell it.'

'Oh, no. We don't have the money for that,' I say, before my dad goes and spends more money we don't have.

'No kidding?' Ramón-Ramona chuckles. 'I realise that, honey, don't you worry. I just need you to look after it for me for a while: eventually I'll sell it.'

'And it's yours?' Pa asks.

'What do you think?' Ramón-Ramona asks, laughing

again. 'Yours too.'

Ramón-Ramona walks away, but leaves the box. When I go to bring it in, I spot Luna: she's wearing a sequined dress, as always, but she's crying. She's crying on the kerb and her extreme, ear-piercing wails shake me to the core.

'Were you out dancing that night?'

'No, Lunita. I wasn't.'

'I was meant to perform. They tied me up,' she says, rubbing her wrists. 'They beat me. They said: "Be grateful we didn't killed you."'

Luna is still weeping, and... How many nights has it been? Two, just two. I think in the past tense, though: in the distant past, so as to drive it far away from me.

★ ★ ★

On the same night the neighbourhood filled with bodies – so many it was like we'd hit upon a forest of bodies – we invited Ramón-Ramona and The Three Toupées to experience, in my dad's words, 'the powers, the great spectacle of The Talking House.'

'Say hello,' he said when we reached the front door, and he quickly pressed play on the tape recorder.

Alirio and Simón dutifully bade the door good evening and, seconds later – quite a few seconds, it seemed to me – we heard my dad's singsong voice.

'Good evening, and welcome! It's me, the door.'

Chickpeas looked at Pa (whose mouth was clamped shut, I suppose to prove to Chickpeas that it wasn't him speaking), then at me, and then at the keyhole. After that he raised his eyebrows and heaved a sigh, as if surrendering.

'The moment you open me,' the recording went on, 'you'll discover the weirdest of worlds. Come on in and see for yourselves, the one, the only, Talking House.'

Pa took out his door keys, but accidentally dropped them. He made frenzied signs at me to pick them up from the ground, and that's what I did, but before I could open the door we were already hearing its voice complain, 'Close me, please. I don't like being left open.'

'But no one's even touched you,' Ramón-Ramona said, looking at the handle with exaggerated earnestness, and then openly mockingly.

'What are you looking at?' the recording went on (these were supposed to be the mirror's lines, in the hallway, but we were still outside). 'Are you looking at yourself or are you looking at me?'

'Open the door,' Pa hissed at me. The lock wouldn't give. 'Open it, come on.'

'Don't just stand there all night,' continued the voice, the mirror. 'Hurry along, now. Don't get caught up seeing yourself in me.'

'I don't get it,' Simón admitted. 'Is it meant to be the house talking?'

'Looks more like his arsehole's doing the talking,' Chickpeas said, staring at the tape recorder ineffectually concealed in my dad's back pocket. 'You've got yourself another idea there, mate: the talking bum, ho, ho, ho… The Blabbering Bumhole.'

'Give me those,' Pa snapped, snatching the keys from me. 'You had one job. I told you a hundred times: timing is everything.'

'But you're the one who dropped the keys…'

'How hard is it to open a door?'

'Hey, no fighting,' Ramón-Ramona intervened. 'If you fight, I'm off.'

'I still don't get it,' Simón said again. 'What is it we're meant to do?'

'You might want to pause the tape,' Chickpeas

suggested, stifling his laughter.

Alirio, meanwhile, was biting his nails. He kept staring out onto the street, but it wasn't clear if he was distracted or trying to concentrate. Then he'd stare at each of us, one by one. Several times, too, he span around suddenly to the house then back to the street. 'Did you hear that?' he kept saying. But we just ignored or talked over him, especially my dad, who was now trying to convince Chickpeas that it was the house, and not he, who was speaking.

Finally, the lock gave. We filed into the house, I'd say not overly enthused about the house tour.

'I'm tired of being on the move,' the recorder said. It was the clock, my dad explained. 'I run and I run and I never stop. I'm tired.'

'This way,' I said, ushering the visitors along, trying to sync up the sound with the objects.

'Yes, come along. This way,' Pa echoed.

We stopped in front of the clock and my dad grew pensive.

'Little clock, little clock, you who marks the time, who knows and represents time, tell me something: has it always existed? Time, I mean. Will it just stop one night?'

Chickpeas couldn't contain a snort, which Ramón-Ramona seconded. My dad chose to ignore them, instead looking at the clock, feigning interest in whatever answer it might give.

'I feel like I'm always chasing people,' the clock replied. 'As if I were hounding them, or pressuring them all the time, telling them: hurry, hurry, hurry, hurry. I don't like that feeling.'

My dad glanced at us, realising he'd asked the wrong question, and quickly corrected himself.

'But tell me, little clock… on time's behalf… have you always existed? Will you simply stop one night…?'

'I, too, ask myself if I've always existed. I can't say if one night I'll simply stop existing.'

'Thank you, clock,' Pa replied.

Our guests burst out laughing. My dad looked at them, perplexed, genuinely curious to know what they were laughing at.

'Let's move on to the kitchen, shall we?' he said, turning a blind eye.

'Watch your step, mister! You trod on me!'

'I'm sorry,' Pa said, looking down at the floor. 'We need a rug.'

'Watch it, watch it!' the tape went on as we walked to the kitchen. 'Don't walk all over me.' When we reached the kitchen, all the visitors still in hysterics, my dad went up to the stove, poured some oil (a dribble) into the pan, lit the hob and began frying an egg.

'It burns, it burns,' moaned the stove, or the egg. 'Does anyone even care if they burn me?'

Ramón-Ramona, meanwhile, was inspecting the drawings my dad had decorated the walls with.

'If you look closely,' Pa explained, 'the egg looks like a lion. The white's his mane. And if you listen closely, you can hear him roar. But I ask you now, ladies and gentlemen, does it just happen to look like a lion, or did the oil, the egg and the frying pan conspire to recreate that great beast? These are questions we cannot help but ask ourselves in this house of wonders.'

'Interesting,' I said, before the others' silence.

And back came the tape (the pan or the egg).

'That burns, it burns. You're burning me.'

'Well, do something! Don't just stand there, you lot,' Simón pleaded, and I couldn't work out whether he was going along with my dad, or whether, who knows, he really did want us to turn off the hob and put the frying pan and the egg out of their misery. Perhaps he just wanted us to stop the tape.

'Wonderful drawings,' Ramón-Ramona said to my dad, looking at him tenderly. 'Did you do them?'

'Yes,' he replied proudly. 'That one at the top is a cow.'

'And this one?'

'Another cow, in the shade of a tree.'

'Well, what do you know,' Chickpeas said. 'I thought it was a cow with a wig on.'

'And all this?' Ramón-Ramona went on, ignoring Chickpeas.

'The stars.'

'And this?'

'My lovely son,' Pa replied, making me blush. I gave him a hug and we stayed like that, hugging, until the egg said, 'I'm ready! You can eat me now.'

'When I've got a bit of money, I'm going to buy you a set of crayons in all different colours,' Ramón-Ramona said.

'Thank you. The black's running low,' Pa replied as he switched off the flame.

'How sad, this life of mine,' the egg concluded. 'To end so soon.'

'We'll eat you later, don't worry,' my dad replied.

We all moved back into the living room and Pa asked us to come over to the window, which we did. Alirio and Simón both seemed distracted. Chickpeas had a little smirk on his face and Ramón-Ramona was yawning, but I was cheery because Pa was no longer angry. Two, three, four seconds later, the recorder began speaking as the window in my dad's now hoarse, almost fluey, voice.

'Outside, the wind is thrashing me.'

'Did you hear that?' Alirio asked. 'What's that noise?'

'The window,' Pa answered. 'It's telling us that the wind outside…'

'No, not that.'

'It sounds like screaming,' I ventured to say, and I felt panic in the pit of my stomach.

The recording, meanwhile, went on.

'Pause it, for fuck's sake,' Chickpeas told Pa. 'Let us listen.'

'Pause what?' he answered, playing dumb.

'Be quiet, man. Just for a second,' Alirio said.

But the recording played on.

'I go and I go and I never stop. I'm tired.'

'Stop it, Pa, please,' I said, losing my patience. I was sure now that there were people screaming outside. 'We're going to have to stop.'

But the tape reran.

'Watch it, watch it!' cried the floor (my dad, his voice). 'Ouch, you're treading on me.'

Exasperated, I launched at Pa.

'Give me that,' I shouted, and I pulled the recorder from his back pocket. In my attempt to stop the tape, I ended up pressing rewind.

'Now look what you've done,' Pa moaned. 'You've ruined everything.'

'Let us listen, man!' Chickpeas said, losing his mind.

'Now no one's going to believe the house can talk.'

'Nobody believed it anyway.'

'You've given the game away.'

'Do you really think anyone believes the house was talking?'

'Well, you never know.'

'They were laughing. They were playing along.'

The Three Toupées and Ramón-Ramona had gone outside. We watched them through the window. They were talking and gesticulating, speculating, perhaps, about what was going on. They were also talking to some of the passers-by.

'Pa,' I said, trying to keep my cool. 'I need to know

you understand that nobody here actually believes the house can talk. They came because you invited them and because you said you wanted to show them strange goings-on. I know you have a plan and that you'd like it, just as I'd like it, if lots of visitors came, but nobody believes that the house really speaks, not for one second. Do you understand that? It's a game. You put it out there and the others decide if they're willing to go along with it or not. The Three Toupées, Ramón-Ramona, they went along with it.'

'I don't know,' my dad said, looking at his feet. 'I suppose I hoped one of them wouldn't work it out and I could show them the tape recorder at the end.'

'They all knew from the start. They went along with it. They were laughing.' There was a pause.

Next thing, Alirio and Ramón-Ramona started waving at us and we went out to join them. They told us what they'd heard. We set off walking. On the corner some men were in tears. One was almost choking, saying, 'Horrible, horrible,' and, 'Oh, God. Oh, God,' and I could feel my eyes opening wide, like his, and drying out. I looked at Pa. I took his hand, stupefied, and wondered how what we were about to see would affect him. And I walked at his side, slowly, my arm around him, glancing over at the Toupées every now and then, and at Ramón-Ramona, who seemed to be walking in slow motion, but at the same time frantically, hurriedly.

There, in the bar district, we came upon men with no heads: four or five bodies, from the neck down, floating in their own lake. Beyond them, in a little heap, the chopped-up crimson flesh of a man (or several men) who'd been out dancing. Another body, across the street, was still in one piece. Blood flowed from one eye into a puddle, and the puddle made a moat around his nose. And his nose, then, seemed to float in the middle of his face.

The street lights, which had been out of action for years, their light bulbs spent, now contained the severed heads in their vitrines. Two of the heads had their mouths agape, their tongues peeping out as if their teeth were the only thing stopping the wet muscle from slipping out entirely. Looking at those heads I imagined, somewhat absurdly, that at some point in the night, light would start pouring from their lantern-lips. Later on, the thought came to me that those lips were radiating darkness.

They'd been inventive: we saw a torso supporting two legs, and not the other way around. We saw arms poking out of other arms, stuffed inside other arms, and cocks and balls hanging from a tree like fruit. There was a man-turned-swing: they'd tied his arms and legs to two posts and he was rocking back and forth, doing the splits, forming a kind of arc. They'd propped another body on top of him: a corpse playing on the swing.

They'd turned others into mannequins, forcing their bruised, gaping bodies to pose down alleyways and on street corners. Some were missing their hands and feet. Others were no more than busts. I recognised several, or so I thought, or so I wanted to believe. Others had had their faces scored out.

The spectacle – yes, the spectacle – continued right down to the park. In the sanded area, where no one went any more, lay the body of a man dressed in white, his eyes inside his mouth and the sockets stuffed with earth. His guts were flowing out of his rectum, not unlike water in a fountain. A dog was lapping them up.

After that, in the square, came the hanged men. Those men-turned-corpses were hanging suspended in the air and seemed to stare impassively at the other corpses before them. And those corpses had been made to look like women. They'd had rocks stuffed down their fronts like breasts. They'd had their penises cut off. Among them hung one whose stomach was moving of its own accord.

'He's alive,' someone said.

But in fact, they'd cut the stomach open and then stitched it back up. Moving closer, we spotted a beak poking in and out of that stomach, grimly pecking at the stitches to make its way out. At last, a cockerel broke free from the fissure and the nameless body fell still.

Last but not least came the impaled. In their semi-present state (of both being and having ceased to be), those bodies on stakes looked like sculptures. Further along, another group were on all fours, arranged in a circle, as if penetrating one another. A little further on, a tree branch – the tree itself – would be raping a body for the rest of time.

'Keep on dancing, butterflies,' they'd written in blood. My dad leant against the wall for a moment. I'm not sure if he accidently pressed the play button, or if it was a conscious decision, but on the way home, walking among the bodies, we heard the recording again, 'Watch it, watch it!' the men-turned-objects seemed to say. 'I'm boiling, I'm burning.'

'What are you looking at?'

'That burns… It's burning me!'

'I run and I run and I run… I'm tired…'

'Close me, please. I don't like being left open.'

'Does no one care that I'm burning?'

'Outside, the wind is thrashing me…'

'Ow! Ow!'

'How sad this life of mine, to end so soon…'

'Hurry along, now. Don't get caught up seeing yourself in me.'

CHAPTER III

Roulette

My dad and I are the only ones left on our block; it's been like this for several nights now. We've noticed some movement further up the street, the odd local who decided to stay, but where we are, in the unlit district, it's just me and him. And sometimes it feels like it's just me, because Pa hasn't left his bed for nights on end, hasn't said a word, hasn't moved. Hour after hour I've watched him slumped on the mattress, vacant-eyed, somewhere else. Little by little, as more people leave the neighbourhood, Pa is growing darker. The disturbances disturbed him; in this new silence he's fallen silent.

Desperately worried about him – about his there-but-not-quite-there state – I try, patiently, to feed him a snack: some stewed fruit, half an egg. Sometimes he eats, sometimes he doesn't. He barely speaks, other than to repeat, 'If we need something from outside, you tell me. You're not going out there. You could get killed.'

Tonight he's no different. I lie down next to him, look at him and smile, in an attempt to cheer him up.

'Let's go to the living room, come on. Stretch our legs a bit,' I say, as I smooth his hair with my palm. He doesn't respond. He doesn't budge. I show him the spoon, with all the enthusiasm I can muster, and open the pot of stewed fruit. He doesn't try any. Then my dad closes his eyes. It's his way of asking me to leave him alone. It's his way of shutting himself off, of shutting me out.

'Eat some,' I say, softly, but he turns away. 'When I come back I want you to have a go,' I insist. 'It's apple, really tasty.'

Back in my room, I sit down on the floor in front of the computer. Every time I do this, I say a little thank you in my head to Ramón-Ramona for having left it with us. There, on the screen, still frozen – hands behind his neck – is the actor who looks like me. I tap the keyboard to unpause the action: the other man, older than him and me by some years, asks him to open his mouth. Stark naked, my double does as he's told, and it seems to me he both resents and relishes being bossed around.

'On your knees,' the older one says to him, yanking his hair. 'Don't even think about putting your hands down.'

So he (I) gets on his knees and, mouth open and hands clasped behind his neck, he waits for the older gentleman's next move. The man unzips his fly and proudly exhibits his flaccid cock.

'Like that, don't you?' he asks the camera, asks him (me). And without waiting for an answer, he puts it in the man's mouth.

I press pause again so I can study the face of the actor, my double. I do it to make a mental note of what I'm like with a cock in my mouth: what I look like, how my face changes. It's truly remarkable how much he looks like me. Seeing him on his knees, pleasuring the other guy, duplicates me: I'm here and I'm there. I'm two bodies. When I unpause and see the older man begin to move, slowly, from the waist down, back and forth, and raise his arms, little by little, enraptured, and hold them there, crossed behind his head, declaring that he can, if he wants, fuck his mouth (my mouth) all night, both my double and I react: our cocks rise, stiffen. Then, his kneeling body (my kneeling body) remains there for another minute, responding to the motion, accepting the motion, obeying the man who can, if he wants, fuck my mouth until the end of the night.

I hear a beep – *the* beep – so I walk around the room with the computer trying to rob some signal. At last it loads.

'Hey,' a window appears. 'What you after?'

I pause the video and concentrate on Roulette: that's the name of the chat room I've been using. The screen is divided into three now. At the bottom is their message to me (and that's where my reply will go, and our exchange, if we strike one up). In the middle there's me, in a frame. And above, in another, there's 'the stranger' (which is the name the chat room gives to the person you meet; so, on the other man's screen, I am 'the stranger'). There's also an arrow between both frames. You click on this arrow to move to the next stranger.

'The idea,' a stranger explained the first time I logged on, 'is that you look at or talk to whoever you want. If you're not into a guy, if you wanna see or talk to someone else, you click the arrow, and if you want you can click again and again until you're too tired to click anymore (hence the name, Roulette), or until you find someone who takes your fancy.'

I adjust my position, watching myself to make sure my face and shoulders are in the frame. I want it to show that I'm not wearing a T-shirt. As for the stranger, he reveals only his torso. You see a lot of headless torsos around here. Then he begins to clutch at his waist, proudly kneading his belly rolls and masturbating at the same time.

'Hey,' I type, and the word appears on the screen, just below my face. 'I've just logged in, where are you?' The man stops wanking and points the camera out of the window to reveal a city I don't recognise.

'And you?'

When I reply, he clicks down.

Next thing, an erection fills the screen. This time it's me who clicks down. Now I can see a man with his back to me, showering. Click: a torso. And another. And one more, hairy this time. Click: there, from the neck down, an old man is sitting and masturbating.

Tired of how few of us show our face, I write to the stranger.

'Hey, you got a face?'

'That depends, man. You got a dick?'

I burst out laughing and click down.

But my dad, the state he's in... I feel bad for having laughed.

* * *

The first time my dad refused to move, refused to leave his bed for nights on end (entire nights spent lying there, asleep or awake, lying there hour after hour in the same position), I dressed up as a butterfly to go to a party. We lived in a block of flats, up on the fifth floor, a long, long way from the sea. And in that tiny space, scarcely lit by the glow of the street lights (and yet dazzled by the starlight, according to Pa), we had a projector that hung from our living-room ceiling and spun round in a continuous slideshow, projecting photos and videos on all four walls. The rapid sequence of scenes (again, according to my dad) lent our humble abode a certain charm, a certain energy, which made it impossible to get bored there.

Our favourite roll mostly contained scenes from my childhood, but also photos of my dad in his 'younger years'. That was his name for a particularly elastic period of his life, which sometimes stretched way beyond my arrival, and at other times ended the night I was born: the exact duration would change depending on my attitude and behaviour. That's how things were, and if for some reason we argued (our arguments were fierce: we'd both end up in tears, not from sadness, but from having shouted so hard and loudly), Pa would wait for a photo to come around in which he appeared alone, without me, younger than I am now (and beautiful, beautiful), doubled over laughing at a party.

'You don't get those years back, that's for sure' he'd say, and then he'd turn to me with, I think, a look of disappointment – feigning a displeasure which I don't think he really felt. Sometimes I'd laugh when he said that and, having ignored him long enough, I'd give him a hug. That was how we always made up. Occasionally, though, I'd snap back, shout at him and slam the door behind me.

'Fine, be alone then,' I'd say, and, defiantly, I'd go out dancing, sometimes into the following evening.

I liked the projector and I liked that it spun around as it produced the images, because it made me think (or feel, maybe) that we were being multiplied in both body and time: my dad and I running along the walls, posing against the walls, smiling from the walls while we wandered around the living room at different ages, watching ourselves move at different ages, in different bodies. We all hung out together in the living room – the men my dad had been, the sons I'd been… Pa and me. Sometimes it pained me to see him like that, radiant on the wall, dancing on the wall, and yet also there in the living room with his head hanging low. Whenever we rowed, my dad would kiss a photo of me as a child and, without looking at me, he'd say, 'I love him, not you.' It hurt, too, to be jealous of myself.

Sometimes, the images landed wherever we happened to be in the living room, which meant the photos were projected not onto the wall but onto our bodies: then, my dad's face, his body, would be cast onto my face (for a second) and my chest and face onto his (for a second), and my body onto his, each cast onto the other, overlapping with each other, my dad me and I him, for a second, cast onto me, cast onto him, for a second, onto each other, onto each other.

'We're broke,' he said as I entered the room in my butterfly costume. 'We're going to have to move.'

I was wearing a pair of white shorts – hot pants, they looked like underwear – and some white sandals with laces that wound up the leg. My mouth, forehead and all around my eyes were daubed in silver glitter, and the rest of my body I'd painted white. A pair of wings, white veils with silvery designs, were fastened to my back and wrists so that if I raised or flapped my arms, they spread out wide into the air. Finally, on my head I wore aluminium antennae foil topped with foil balls.

'Things are bad,' my dad continued when I didn't respond.

'How bad?'

'Bad, bad. We'll have to move.'

'Move when? Move where?'

'Further down Lights Avenue.'

'But where?'

'We'll have to see, I don't know yet.'

But my dad did know, and I knew that he knew. And I resented him not telling me, just as I resented finding out how poor we were out of the blue like that, with no warning.

'Why didn't you tell me any of this before?' I shouted, and then I spread my wings and stormed off to my party, slamming the door behind me and leaving him all alone.

★ ★ ★

For the most part, conversations on Roulette are mechanical. The strangers ask what I'm after, what I'm into, where I am, and sometimes my age. I answer, then ask the same questions back. If my face is in the frame and you can tell I'm topless, they ask me to show my cock. If I'm wanking and my cock is in the frame, they ask me to show my face. Never, at the start of a chat, have I shown my face and cock at once. Lots of people do the same, presumably for fear that someone will take a screenshot. That is, for fear that someone will do exactly what I've been doing all these nights.

I, on the other hand, am not worried about ending up frozen in a frame, naked on the other man's computer screen. If I don't show my whole body from the start, or when they first ask, it's because I want to prolong the pleasure of being seen first in parts (my face, my chest) and then as a whole.

I click the arrow down. The stranger, a chubby man more or less my age, opens his mouth and moves in towards the camera. Then he sticks out his tongue and puts his fist in his mouth.

'Your mouth fits all that?' it occurs to me to ask him. I take a screenshot and click down before saving the scene in a file I call 'My collection'.

The next one types something.

'Well, don't you look pretty.'

He's a faceless torso – another one – and he sends me a transcript of moans.

'Ooh, ah, oh.' He tells me to move back from the camera so he can see my chest. I do as he says and then he writes, 'Now rub it, rub yourself, give it to me,' and again, I do as he says. I rub my chest, my hair… I run my hands all over myself and the man writes, 'That's it, like that, like that,' before tilting his camera down to show me his erection.

The video freezes. Whenever this happens I notice a new expression: either my own or the stranger's. I like seeing myself reflected in the other man's gaze, studying myself in the other's gaze and being surprised, too, by my own. I like learning my own expressions.

★ ★ ★

I walked along Lights Avenue with my back to the sea, heading deeper into the electric forest. The street lights, their yellow light, multiplied as I went. Light, light and more light. So much light that, instead of illuminating the night or dissipating the darkness, it seemed to create them: the brightness underscored the night, and the dark felt extreme when set against such profuse, opulent light.

Lights Avenue was straight, but intersected with other roads that spiralled up off the ground, rising into the air and becoming bridges. Those metres and metres of suspended concrete, which sometimes interlaced like strings or noodles (bridges joining other bridges, streets over streets over streets), always ran back down to the earth, maybe a little sad to land, or maybe relieved. And I liked looking at the cars at night driving up and down each road, going so fast they seemed to become a blaze of light, or a gust of wind crackling with sparks.

It was easy to be dazzled, to live in a state of bedazzlement. As well as all that light there was the brightness of the screens. And the camera flashes. The screens lit up the façades of endless rows of building, filling the night with fizz and sparkle: beer cans opening of their own accord, unleashing a frothy, fluorescent white foam; models instantly changing from outfit to outfit (a jacket and tie – flash – underwear, a swimsuit – flash – shorts and a shirt); plenty of mouths, too, sipping through straws an assortment of liquids, several of them black; and words, words that appeared and disappeared again: *love, buy, come, eat, drink, more*... Each word a colour, a flare lit in the dark. On top of all the adverts came the short sharp bursts of camera shots. I especially liked seeing people's faces, their poses when photographed. The night I went out partying, several passers-by wanted to take their picture with me.

'Look at that guy!' they said. 'The butterfly.' And they came over, smiling, saying, 'Photo, photo!' and *flash*. They thanked me and left, delighted, ready to carry on posing: with the city, with those around them.

And the city's extravagance was compounded by how extravagant the people in it were: it amazed me how at odds all that eccentricity was with the robotic way they walked. That very night I saw a man walking with a cat on his head (and for a moment I wondered if the cat was real or stuffed, but then it meowed, I think when it noticed me staring, perhaps sensing my curiosity). I saw a woman dressed in a freshly polished suit of armour, walking her pig (and the pig was wearing a top hat). Another woman was wearing a costume made of glass and flowers. And another had mannequin hands sitting on each of her shoulders.

Someone was shouting, someone singing. Someone else was crying down the phone, asking 'What? What?' and 'How?' and then crying some more. That night, lots of the lamp posts had the same flyer pinned to them, 'Come and let off... Steam' (and an address underneath).

Overhead, aeroplanes cut through the night sky, one after another, and I let myself go with them, far, far away: a different journey with each plane, never the same. And what noise those dots of red light made in the fog! Each time I heard one I felt sure it was nearby. At the same time I thought how impressively loud the sound must be, to be heard from so far away.

Disco buses also filed past; and with them, more lights in motion, more colour. And music, too, sounding loudly: untz, untz, untz, wub, wub, untz, untz. 'All aboard the party bus!' came the indiscriminate cries from heads hanging out of the bus windows. And it was generally pedestrians, like me, who accepted the impromptu invitation to those mobile parties. 'Oh yeah!' the heads would bellow if someone hopped on. 'Shake your body, get those hips moving'. And untz, untz.

As all of this took place and shone (I felt that in the city 'existing' and 'shining' were the same thing), I thought about Pa's news and repeated his words to myself.

'We're going to have to move.'

And even as I thought the thought, I put it out of my head, giving in to the distraction of the buildings in the electric forest, which were vying it out in a competition to see which was tallest. Many of the buildings had reflective façades; and those mirrors reflected the other buildings, magnifying the immensity of it all.

There was a long queue when I finally reached the party venue: a multi-storey car park with bars and dance floors set up here and there, and lights (more lights), and luxury cars too, each one with its doors open so we could get inside. I was still thinking about the news when I reached the end of the queue, and about Pa left all alone when I'd slammed the door behind me ('Where to?', 'I don't know', 'Things are bad, really bad'…). And as I thought about that, I looked at all the costumes around me: hordes of men in their underpants, posing as models or dandies with the ruffled bedhead look; lots of birds. Someone clutched his cock and yelled, 'This is my one true God!' He was dressed as a bear, a teddy bear, and everyone around applauded.

A man, one of the birds, came over to tell me, 'I like your costume'. I smiled and winked, although in my head I was still thinking, 'Things are bad'. The man spoke, we spoke, but I wasn't really listening.

'See you inside?' he asked, searching out my eyes (and patting my nipple).

'I dunno, I don't think so. The queue's not moving,' I replied before saying goodbye and walking off, now with my back to the electric forest.

★ ★ ★

Roulette springs back to life: two kids sing and blow kisses at me. I blow one back, and they make little heart signs with their hands. I smile and they wave goodbye and click down.

'Hi,' the next stranger writes, and he waves a revolver in front of the camera.

'What's with the gun?' I ask, with some trepidation.

The mouth smiles.

'To kill you with.'

And then, a vision: the heads in the street lights. Before I get the chance to write something, anything, the mouth – the stranger – clicks down.

★ ★ ★

I passed our building. It occurred to me to go up and talk to my dad, but I carried on without stopping. That's what I wanted to do – to follow the route of a stream that formed out of rainfall and flowed down to the sea. The street lights were becoming scarcer; with each step, it grew darker. Something caught my attention on a street corner: a man, his restive movements – he glanced over his shoulder twice, as if to check nobody was there, before heading into a bar. He must have seen me (he couldn't not have seen me), which led me to think that it didn't bother him that I, in particular, saw what he was doing. I walked towards the door and saw that the place was called Steam. I remembered what it was (the flyer on the lamp posts), and I went in.

There were two men in the queue – or three, including me. I decided to stay. The second one, the man I'd seen on the street, turned around when I stood behind him, and looked at me maliciously, I felt, as if my joining the queue had confirmed his suspicions.

'Next,' someone called.

'Next,' said someone else.

The men went to the cabin and began speaking into a grille.

'I'll take a room,' the first man said.

'One locker,' said the second.

They paid, I couldn't see how much, and in return received a towel and some keys. Then they disappeared off through a door, which was wet with condensation.

'Next,' they called. I smiled at the man behind the glass – bald, with gold or gold-plated teeth – and asked him for a locker.

'First time?' he asked me.

'Yeah,' I replied and he passed me a key and towel.

'It's on the house this time,' he went on. 'So you come back…' The man handed me a second towel, saying I'd need it, and added, 'Lockers are on the left.'

The first thing I saw when I opened the door were three more doors. Men were walking in and out of them, pacing around watchfully, with only their towels wrapped around their waists. Some were openly eyeing each other up, while others avoided eye contact but at the same time glanced sidelong at the men around them, approaching this one or that, looking each other up and down. The main room, and everything in it, was black – the floor, the ceiling, the walls were all in stark contrast to the bright white towels. A flashing strip of red light ran around the doors and the spiral staircase, which was at the back; the light, that is, showed us the paths we could follow inside.

As I looked for my locker, I saw a man putting a hand on the leg of another, who had blue hair; the second man brushed the hand straight off, as if brushing away a fly, and continued on his way. Another guy, younger, did the same thing: very gently, one hand on the leg; and then the other hand, running through the blue hair. They stood there like that, staring at one another… then, a kiss. Next thing, the rejected man was back. He found a column and leaned against it, settling in for the show. The men removed their towels – each other's – and, still kissing, began to tug each other off. The one leaning against the column also removed his towel to start wanking along with them. Every now and then the couple stopped kissing, interrupting the kiss to stare at the lone man, without stopping touching each other: in that way, they both included and excluded him.

I watched them, and I watched him watching them. I saw myself in them and in him. And there and then I understood the codes of the place: we were in a labyrinth, and we, the men inside it, were doors, walls and mirrors. Paths, in and of ourselves, every one of us. Tunnels, in the end. Tunnels.

★ ★ ★

Click. I'm looking for the man with the gun. Click, click, click.

'Have you chatted to a man with a gun?' I ask the stranger, whose nipple is a sun with rays tattooed around the areola.

'You want me to show you a shooter?' the man asks me in turn, and he lowers the camera to reveal his cock.

I click the arrow down and ask the next man the same question.

'Have you spoken to a man with a gun?'

'No,' says the torso on the screen.

Click.

'Talk dirty to me,' a beer belly says.

I click down, but it reappears.

'Tell me you're going to get me blind drunk and give it to me hard tonight.' I click, and copy and paste my question.

'Have you chatted to a man with a gun?'

At last, the cock on the screen answers 'Yes.' And then, a memory: the cockerel, its beak, pecking its way out of the body.

'Did he say anything to you?' I ask, but the camera starts to zoom out. Now the stranger with no body hair reveals himself from the neck down. He turns around, opens wide, and slides his finger in and out. On the other side of his window, far, far away, I see another city. And then, another image flashes before me: the man penetrated by the branch of a tree.

I close Roulette and leave my room. I look at my dad, who is still slumped on the mattress. I kiss him, give him a little shove. I say, 'Pa, come on, get up,' but he doesn't respond, his open eyes look straight through me. And then, another vision: the blood on the wall, the message, 'Keep on dancing, butterflies.'

* * *

In the locker room I took off my wings, antennae and shorts. I considered leaving my sandals on when I looked at the black floor, repulsed, imagining it would feel sticky, but in the end I opted to take them off too. Every now and then I thought about my dad, and the news. 'We're in trouble, real trouble. We're going to have to move.' When, where to? My dad knew and he didn't want to tell me.

I ended up in nothing but a towel, though my face and body were still covered in glitter and white face paint. I left my costume in the locker, along with the second towel. I tied the key to my wrist and began to walk around, vigilant, like everyone else: staring, in search of who knows what. In search of everything.

I came to the three doors, and, exactly as I'd thought, it was a labyrinth. On opening the first one, I found even more. A narrow corridor, with doorway after doorway: ways in (ways out). At the end there was a mirror which made the corridor appear longer, and duplicated the men who walked past. Some disappeared through those doors; some came out. And others just stood on the threshold, waiting, I guessed, for more men.

I closed that door and opened the next one – some guys just walked through, brushing past me. There was steam inside. I couldn't see a thing, so I went in. More steam. I took a few tentative steps, to get used to the whiteness. Faces and arms came out of nowhere (or so it seemed), as if detached from the rest of the bodies, floating in the mist. Lots of people were walking with their arms out in front of them to avoid colliding with walls or undesirable bodies; and, also, to touch the desirable bodies. You could hear moaning.

I was sweating profusely in there – 'The Wet Zone', it was called. Sometimes they sprayed water from the ceiling, to cool us down. They also turned on the lights every now and then for a few seconds, and then it all became clear: the way ahead, the faces. We stared at each other. And yet the light also made us freeze on the spot: nobody moved a muscle until the lights were off again.

And with the bodies hazy once more, we loosened up again. I saw a man kneel down before another man. I watched him remove the second one's towel and raise his hands up to his head as if letting himself go. And I liked that: how he just let himself go.

I came to a door, unsure if it was the same one I'd come in through, and I left.

'Look at the kid', a bearded man said. 'Cream-pied!'

I heard titters and turned around to see who was talking, who was laughing. To my surprise, I found they were laughing at me: the water, the steam, had soaked the face paint, which was now dripping – white, thick and gleaming – down my chin and chest. I rolled my eyes. More laughter.

Turning my back on them, I saw a man open the third door: the walls and all the lights in this room were red. It looked like the source of all the red light that delineated the labyrinth. In the middle of the room, hanging from the ceiling, was a swing, and I could just make out that the seat was made of leather and suspended from metal chains.

'There's no one in there now,' one man said, looking at another, at anyone, 'but it'll soon fill up.' And with that, he closed the door. The men from before – there were four of them – were still laughing and staring at me.

'Butterfly, butterfly!' someone shouted. It was the guy I'd seen outside, before entering the labyrinth. He came over, sneering, a small glass bottle in his hand, his eyes wide open like claws.

'Where did you leave that costume of yours?' he taunted.

'You're the one who came in wearing wings?' one of the jeering men chipped in. I looked over but ignored him.

'Yeah, that's him,' the other one said, and he laughed. More turned up. 'What's so funny?' they asked.

'No, nothing, just that our friend here likes to fly.' They cracked up.

'Uh oh, risky!' I heard someone say, and then they all started crying out, 'Butterfly, butterfly!'

Then they were dancing, jigging up and down. They linked arms to form a circle and bobbed their heads from side to side. One of the men jumped into the middle to dance alone. He put his hands on his hips and pouted. He came to life, mechanically.

I made a mental note of their faces and went looking for the showers.

'Butterfly!' they went on shouting. 'Butterfly!'

★ ★ ★

That memory steers me to another: of me as a child, jumping and singing, waving my arms – my wings – and trying to fly. And of a man who comes towards me nodding and saying, 'That's it! That's it, fly!' In my memory it's both for him and for myself that I keep on trying. I spot a flat tyre in the street, stand on top of it and launch myself upwards. For a few seconds, I'm high in the air, and when I come down I bounce back up, flapping my hands. I'm flying.

All the while the man keeps clapping.

'Fly. That's it, fly!' he cries, and, with him (for him) I revel in my airborne lightness. 'Fly, fly!'

But then his expression changes. His face turns red, angry and grimacing. 'Fly, fly!' says the voice. And then, more men: they look at me, at each other... a commotion ensues.

'Fly away, fly away!' the stranger calls out, as if in a trance, and then finally he yells, incensed, 'Butterfly!'

My face paint was still dripping.

The showers were at the other end of the locker room, arranged in a circle. There was no wall to separate the soap-lathered men from the rest: the showers formed an integral part of the labyrinth, and as they showered, the men presented – indeed they *were* – something of a spectacle.

When I reached the showers, two young boys were standing under the jets of water. Each was looking down at the ground, and every now and then they threw their heads back with their eyes shut tight. The water pounded down onto their foreheads and necks... It seemed the water was cooling them off.

From outside, a group of men were watching them, their eyes fixed on those freshly clean bodies – renewed bodies, ready for more sex. I removed my towel but, before I could reach the circle, an old guy approached me, grabbed my arm and shook me.

'What do you think you're doing?' he asked, leering at me.

I looked at him, bewildered, afraid even. Then the old man smiled and I heard him say, 'Give me some of that,' as he began to lick my chest.

'It's make-up,' I said.

* * *

'This stewed fruit is really good,' I repeat, 'or would you rather I fry you a runny egg?'

Faced with my dad's silence, I resort to jokes.

'Don't tell me you want to play Here Comes the Aeroplane.'

I raise the spoon to make it fly: the mixture eddies

and swirls in the air before him. 'Open up,' I say. 'Here comes the aeroplane.'

My dad clamps his mouth shut.

Back again on the floor of my room, I log into Roulette. There I am in the frame, a fragment: a close-up of my cock.

'Are you close?' a man writes. 'Go on, beautiful. Finish.'

There's something about the way he looks at me that excites me: his hunger. He bites his lip and locks his eyes on me, on the screen.

'You ever show your face on here?'

I carry on wanking, so he insists.

'Don't be a meanie, let me see it.'

I begin to draw back the camera. The man moves in closer. Now, in this frame, you can only see eyes – his eyes, and part of his forehead. In my frame, my body slowly starts to appear, from my knees up to my neck. I take a screenshot.

'More,' the man goes on. 'Zoom out some more. I want to see your face when you come.' I draw back the camera a little further, and as I do, the man's eyes begin to open wide. 'That's it, like that. Faster.'

You can see my mouth now. I open it and moan as I tug at my cock.

'Mmm,' the stranger types. He points his camera down to show me his bent dick before raising it again to reveal his wide-open eyes.

I continue slowly drawing back the camera to reveal myself. Half my face, now – the mouth and nose. I go on wanking. The man, I sense, is biting his lip even harder.

'Oh yeah, oh yeah. That's it,' he writes. And I draw back the camera… I'm almost showing my eyes, my whole face. 'Go on, come. Gimme cream.' I draw it back a little. A little further and… 'Faster, go on. Face and cock, go on.'

I click down.

It's not that I'm cruel. I just want to make him hungrier.

★ ★ ★

I stood under the shower a long while. I lathered myself in soap several times, partly to clean off the glitter and body paint, and partly to postpone going back out into the labyrinth. The other bathers, both of them, tried to catch my eye. I looked at them and smiled, but went on washing. One of them spoke up.

'I'm in 200, first door on the right,' he said, before leaving the circle of showers to dry off.

'I'll be there,' I replied, and the man smiled.

The younger man (the younger of the two, and yet still older than me) turned off the tap and sidled under another shower: now he was directly next to me. He turned on the tap and moved to face me. He massaged his scalp for a few seconds, flashing his clean-shaven armpits. Then something – *something*: a tingling, that throbbing in my cock.

More men appeared. They hung around on the edge of the circle, watching, waiting to see if anything would happen. I closed my eyes to think, above all about what I wanted, or what I was prepared to do in there. And yet my mind remained blank. I opened my eyes and saw that the younger one – erect, more handsome now – was still looking at me. I looked at him, he looked at me and he looked down at his cock. In that way, he guided me to it.

I moved in and our mouths met. I gulped great mouthfuls of water as we kissed. He put his hands on my shoulders, first squeezing them, and then pushing down, pushing me down to my knees. The warm water was drenching me, and his cock... for a moment I saw it up close, the shining, pink head; the shaft was pink too, although paler, and you could see veins pulsing along it. And those veins... Before putting his cock in my mouth, I caught sight of the guy's face, looking down at me from above: he seemed patient in the certain knowledge of what was about to happen. Out of the corner of my eye I also saw the other men, our audience.

I closed my eyes again and opened my mouth, which the guy then filled. I wrapped my lips over my teeth to avoid biting him. In moving my neck I moved my head, and in moving my head I swallowed his cock, then spat it out, and then swallowed it again. Sometimes water rushed in, the warm water still running down my body. And sometimes I swallowed the water, like I swallowed his cock, and sometimes I spat it out.

'Wait,' the guy said, and he turned off the tap. He took a towel – his or mine – and began to dry himself. There were more spectators now, several of them masturbating. 'That's better,' the guy said. 'All dry.' And with one hand he pinched my cheeks (opening my mouth), and with the other he took his cock. He began wanking too: he flitted between looking at the other men and at me. He was still going, and I was turned on by the thought that I was about to taste another man's cum for the first time.

'It's taking me a while,' he said, and I went down on him again. And this time I wanted to look at him as I did it. I ran my tongue over the head, I tasted his balls; I looked up to watch him watching me.

He drew away a little and resumed tossing himself off, this time more vigorously. He was about to come, he was about to come... his cock was slowly changing colour: from pink to puce to purple. He was moaning, and the other men were moaning along with him. I opened my mouth and knelt there waiting for him, looking at him: he seemed tired.

The guy got up.

'I'm sorry, I can't,' he said, and he took the towel, covered himself and left the circle. I was left alone, on my knees in the showers before the crowd. A man let out a loud moan, announcing he'd come: a disappointing white squirt on his belly.

★ ★ ★

'What's a pretty boy like you doing on here?' the stranger asks.

I don't want to tell him that, for several nights in a row now, I've spoken only to men on Roulette. I click the arrow down and think about my dad, about the last time he looked out of the window. His only words were, 'Still life.'

An empty bed appears on the screen. Click: an arse, now, filling the frame. The stranger, bending over, prises open his arsehole. He sticks a finger in and then slides it out again. Click: a man with a white beard.

'Hey, I'm all yours,' I write.

The man smiles and raises his eyebrows.

'You'll do whatever I want?'

'Yeah.'

'Let me think.'

I lean back against the wall with my hands behind my head like pillows. I wait. Finally, the stranger writes something.

'I tell you what, you tell me what *you'd* want us to be doing if we were in the same place.'

I'd imagined that I'd have to humour his whims, step by mechanical, obedient step, so I'm taken aback. I'm also confronted with a challenge: to turn him on using words. And with a gamble: whatever I write might turn him off.

I look at Roulette. I'm showing my face and torso. I am − and more to the point, I appear − stark naked. He, on the other hand, has his shirt buttoned up.

'Show me your room,' I say.

The stranger obeys and pans the room: on the left there's a sofa; on the right, two chairs. There is also a table in the middle of the room with a tall pile of books and a vase on it. The windows in the background have curtains that are wide open and lead the eye out to sea.

'I'd knock on the door,' I begin, 'and you'd tell me to make myself at home because you're not ready. I come in and sit on the sofa. I'm wearing a white, cotton T-shirt. Shorts, sandals. It's hot. Not long after, you come out of your bedroom smelling of aftershave. You're wearing a long-sleeved black shirt and grey trousers. We kiss.'

'Uh huh,' the stranger replies indifferently.

Determined to get him going, I continue.

'You take off my shorts, then my T-shirt. We're still kissing…'

'Are you naked or wearing underpants?'

'I'm in tight, white little boxers.'

'Aha.'

'And you say precisely these words: "You're so undressable…"'

'Do I touch you through your boxers?'

'Yes. And then you take them down.'

'You're so undressable,' he jokes.

I tip the camera down and show him my body.

'You do this,' I write, running my free hand over my torso. 'And then…' I hesitate. What's the best word to use? Do I write 'cock', 'dick'? Do I write 'horny for you'? I say, 'You start to suck my cock. You slide your finger in, you run your tongue up and down my arse crack. I'm really horny for you.'

'Aha.'

'And you kiss my armpit too.'

'When do I take off my clothes?'

'You don't. I want to be naked but also to feel naked. If you take off your clothes I won't feel naked.'

'OK.'

'In the meantime, you ask me: "What do you like? What do you want me to do?" And I tell you, "Pin my arms up, kiss me."'

'Aha.'

'And you ask me, "What else?" and I say, "Finger me without taking your eyes off me", and, "Kiss me, play with my cock,"... And so, with your questions, you strip me even more naked. You like the fact that, even though I'm already naked, I become more and more nude.'

'Yeah.'

'Then you lift up my legs and...'

The stranger clicks down.

★ ★ ★

I left the showers and went wandering around.

In the red room an old man was now on the swing. He was naked – waiting – with his legs wide open. The seat was long, almost a hammock, so going on the swing actually implied lying down on it. The old man craned his neck every now and then, and whenever anyone walked past, he opened his legs even wider.

Every time someone looked away on seeing him, or every time a group of men all together ignored him, the man glanced at his watch.

★ ★ ★

'Where are you?' the torso asks me.

Click: an old man is snoring in a seat.

'Sir, you're better off on the bed,' I write, hoping the message might make a sound. The stranger, however, doesn't wake up.

I return to my dad.

Lying on the bed I touch, or rather stroke, his cheeks. I ask him if he has a fever; I tell him he doesn't have a fever. I leave the room, leaving him. But straight away I hate myself, take pity on him, and go back.

My dad looks at me, empty, as I look at him and feel myself emptying out. He closes his eyes when I plead with him to get up. Then I try to lift him: I hook my arms under his armpit and heave, but I fall on top of him and it's my dad who ends up carrying me. I look at him and he avoids my gaze. He falls asleep, or pretends to.

'I'll be back in a second,' I say, and head to the bathroom. There, written across the mirror, is the word 'God'. And I don't know if it's endearing or terrifying that my dad has scrawled 'God' in sprawling black writing on the mirror, either looking at or for himself in the reflection.

★ ★ ★

I returned, quite accidentally, to the corridor of doors. I could feel eyes on me, and how the men held their gaze steady if they liked what they saw, or turned away if they didn't. I stole the odd glance at them, and did the same: if I liked them, I'd keep staring; if I didn't, I'd avoid their eyes (and, in doing so, avoid an encounter with them).

I left the corridor, tired of seeking – tired, too, of being sought. I ended up in a room, alone, and decided to stay there, watching a video being shown across three TV screens: a close-up of a belly button full of spunk.

I sat down on a long, leather sofa, bemused by the image before me. The shot slowly zoomed out to reveal a spurting cock, and a hand wrapped around it. Next thing, a man appeared: both in the room and on the screens. The man in the room sat down to watch me. The one in the video went on choking the dick, which wasn't his own. He tugged and even slapped it.

The man in the room stretched out one of his feet and touched mine. I looked at him, and he came over. On the screens, meanwhile, a boy was shouting, 'Stop, no more, stop'. He was tied to a chair, and despite his cries, the man went on squeezing and tugging – the boy had already come, but the man went on wanking him off.

It all happened very quickly: on the sofa we kissed, both of us sitting down. After a second, the man stood up in front of me. We started wanking each other off: me him first, for a moment, then him me. And every now and then I looked up at him and to watch the screen.

'I'm gonna come,' I said, but before I could, he came on my stomach. I followed, pressing my eyes shut, then shuddering. On the screen the boy was shouting, 'No more, please, no more,' but the man went on torturing him, smiling.

A kiss. I opened my eyes, we said goodbye. I thought later that the man had been handsome. And yet, even as I thought it, his features blurred with the faces of other men.

I decided to take a shower – another one. Searching for them, lost in the labyrinth, I came across a mirror. I liked the vision of myself all covered in cum, and now, finally, unable to tell whose cream was whose.

* * *

'One for you and one for me, what do you think?' My dad nods and opens his mouth. He tries some stewed fruit, and swallows it indifferently. I say well done, and give him a kiss. I take the next mouthful, and he the following one. And we keep going like that for some time.

Afterwards, back in the other room, I receive a message from a backlit face.

'Do me a favour: roll up a pillow and put your cock in it. Show me how you'd move if you were fucking me.'

'I'll show you how I'd fuck you without any pillow,' I write before getting on my knees with my face in the camera and making a circle with my closed hand. I put my cock in him. I put my cock in my closed fist, gently at first so it doesn't hurt, and taking care not to move the hand but my body. I'm not wanking; this is sex. I thrust my hips back and forth and the stranger readjusts the light: he's almost a kid. I look him in the eyes, looking into the camera. I want him to feel my eyes on him. I want him to know that I'm looking at him and focusing on him while I'm inside.

His expression is one of pleasure but also surprise. It's the face of someone who didn't expect to get what he asked for. I get on all fours and throw my head back. I open my mouth in a *o* shape. I keep thrusting. I move in and out of his arse − my hand − until he says, 'Stop. My turn.' And then he rolls up a pillow, licks his lips, and reproduces all of my moves.

I take a photo − of him, of the scene, which includes me − and save it straight to my collection, with my other screenshots.

'Arse. Show me it,' he writes, and again I do as he says. I keep one eye on myself in the frame the whole time: there I am, lying down with my legs open. Sometimes I look awkward, or insecure, and sometimes, I'm brimming with me.

★ ★ ★

More passages led off from the corridor of doors, and more doors ran along each of them. Many were closed, but I was able to poke my head around the ones left ajar and sneak a look at the men inside: naked old men, draped across beds, snoring loudly; young guys on their knees, their backs to the door, spreading their arse cheeks with both hands; men screwing, calling others to join them and turn their twosomes into threesomes, their threesomes into orgies.

At one of these intersections, a man – 'Teddy', a guy walking by called him – told me to follow him. And that's what I did, sure of both him and myself. We turned left down another corridor, and then went straight, or turned right, and then straight again, left, right, straight. We came to a room similar to the one I'd been in earlier. Or was it the same one? There was a large leather sofa in there, and on the walls, some TV screens showing movies. In one of them, a naked man was suspended from the ceiling, and another guy, dressed in a suit and tie, was kissing him and wanking off.

The man, Teddy, removed my towel then lunged at me and we fell crashing onto the sofa. He looked at me and kissed me, wanking at the same time, not taking his eyes off my face. At one point, though, he put his hand on my chin, lifted it, and began inspecting my face, turning it from side to side. He alternated between touching me and touching himself studying me all the while.

Then the man began to mould my face with his hand, as if making little modifications; as if trying, I felt, to make me look like someone else. He stretched my forehead taut, pulling my eyes open. He squished my cheeks in a little, and pushed my eyebrows together. And apparently, like that, with my eyebrows closer in, I managed to look like the person he wanted me to be. All the while he was squeezing my brow like that, Teddy went on wanking.

He came on my dick and said goodbye with a 'Thanks'.

★ ★ ★

'Hey,' writes the stranger (really just a hairy belly), 'where are you?'

I click the arrow down. And again.

'Where are you?'

Click. The next one, who has black eyes and green hair, proposes we talk. 'Sure,' I reply, and he smiles, happily or incredulously, I can't tell. He explains that he's wanted to talk to someone since he entered the chat room hours ago, but that everyone, sooner or later, ends up asking him to strip.

'I can do talking', I say, to which he replies, straight away, 'Awesome, where are you?'

Bored of the question, I put Roulette on pause.

I decide to go through 'My collection'. It's already seventy pages long. I look at the photos, the screenshots – every stranger frozen just once, and me, frozen with every stranger. I scroll quickly through the pages and enjoy the effect of each man melding into the next, or into mere body parts, as I also shift about: moving closer or further away, wanking, getting on all fours, on my back, on my front, opening my mouth, staring into the camera. A hundred men in one; a stranger transforming into a hundred strangers. All of them interchangeable, apart from me.

Faced with this multitude, I realise that it excites me more seeing my own naked, moaning self than any of the others. I ask myself, not without some regret, why that might be. I look at them. I look at myself... It's a cycle: I look into their eyes, which are looking at my body, which is fixed in their gaze. In the end, the strangers – their gaze, their hundred gazes – fall back on me.

Frustrated, I unpause the page. Click.

I call out to my dad in the other room.

'You have to get out of bed and move your legs a little!'

★ ★ ★

I resumed my search for the showers. In one of the corridors, towards the last door, I saw a man: he was standing against the light and I liked his physique. I walked towards him, determined to talk to him or catch a glimpse of his face, and hoping something might happen between us. He came towards me too, hesitant at first, as if peeling his feet from the floor. But when I picked up my pace, he did the same, moving closer. Both of us drew closer and closer, until... a mirror.

★ ★ ★

Click. The stranger asks me to pull faces at him.

'What kind of faces?' I ask.

'Faces, funny faces. Like this,' he says, and starts jerking his head back and forth robotically, puffing out his cheeks. He rolls his eyes, sticks out his tongue, flairs his nostrils. And from his face, he seems to be making noises too, 'Gua, fua, rua,' and 'Mu, fu, tu.' He's getting increasingly excited: he pulls one ear, then both together. He bares his teeth in a frozen roar.

'Faces,' he types. 'Pull faces for me. They turn me on.' I go to pull a face and... I can't do it. Click.

★ ★ ★

At last, I found the showers. There, on either side of the room, two separate orgies were going on. On one side, eleven, maybe twelve men were penetrating another five or six. Lying down or on his knees, each one was receiving in either his mouth or his arse – in a few cases, two cocks to a single orifice. On the other side, the men were sucking each other off in a circle. Several of them also spread themselves open to receive.

When I went in to shower, I witnessed something at once completely foreseeable and completely unbelievable. Two men on all fours, their eyes meeting, each from the other orgy, but crawling, slowly, towards one another, without pulling away from whoever was penetrating them. And like that, they drew the rest of the men with them, and the two orgies came together in a kiss.

★ ★ ★

On the screen, a dripping vibrator.

'That brown there,' I write to the stranger, 'is it chocolate or shit?'

The camera pans out and a man with a buzz cut appears, smiling.

'Shit, of course,' he writes, and he puts the vibrator in mouth, staring into the camera. I'm repulsed, and yet… I wet my bottom lip, bite it, making out as if I were lapping up the image. Clearly shocked, the man clicks down.

★ ★ ★

As I showered, a man came on another man's face; another moved in and out of another; and another, flaccid, began tossing himself off, grew erect and started fucking another.

In that place, sex was always going on, just at different stages.

★ ★ ★

I think about my dad, and go back to lie down beside him ('beside him' is code for spooning him).

'Pa, that's enough. Come on, we're getting out of here. Don't be like this anymore.'

Nothing.

I sigh. My eyes dim. Then a thought hits me. I open my eyes, and… No. No.

'Pa?'

I shoot off the bed, shaking. No, no. I take a step back and look at him before leaning in.

'Pa?'

I put my hand to his mouth and… he's breathing.

★ ★ ★

I trod on a lot of condoms as I wandered, lost, around the labyrinth. At first I found the feeling of the oily rubber repugnant, but I soon got used to it, and eventually there was no meld of lube and shit that could repulse me.

On several occasions that night, I entered a room, or a corridor, and two, or sometimes three men would start to trail me. If I turned around and spoke to one of them, the other, or the others, would stop to listen in. But they'd remain silent, just staring. And whenever someone new showed up, he'd ask, 'And you lot? What you up to?' To which someone else would reply, 'Nothing yet.'

And if I kissed the stranger, or the stranger kissed me, others would approach and then more would begin to crowd around us. The odd one here or there would stretch out his arms to touch us, the ones in the middle.

And yet, in that constellation of men, those of us in the middle would end up pushed to the sidelines strangely fast. Another couple would arrive, or another man, and then everyone would turn their back on the centre, forming a new centre in the process. Those of us who had been surrounded had to decide at that point if we wanted to carry on screwing, or if our encounter had been contingent upon the presence of the audience.

We almost never carried on screwing.

* * *

Back on Roulette again, a stranger is fondling his chest. With his right hand he wanks, but he soon switches position, tossing himself off with his left hand, touching himself – his arse crack, his neck –, pinching his nipples. Next thing he stops wanking, runs both hands back over his chest, clasps his neck. Then he moves them down to his anus, showing it to me, putting his finger in and smelling it before starting to wank again. Finally, he moves his hands back up, this time to his armpits, showing them off to me, fondling them.

'You need more hands.' I write.

* * *

In the wet zone, drifting through the steam, I spotted a man. And on seeing him, I went cold. I crept along behind him to confirm my suspicions, but soon lost him in the miasma. When I spotted him again, I thought, 'It's him, it's him,' and I continued to follow him. He disappeared briefly and then I saw him again.

'Pa?' I called out, but the man carried on his way.

'Pa?' I repeated, and the man turned around.

'Sorry, kid. I'm way too young for that game.'

* * *

71

'How is it possible?' an old man writes. 'A young thing like you in a place like this?'

I tilt the camera down and start to masturbate.

'You like older men?'

'Yeah.'

'Why?'

I click down.

★ ★ ★

As I left the wet zone, I spied a man fucking another man. The receiver, tall and lanky, was clean-shaven from head to toe. The giver, robust and much older, was whispering in his ear.

'You feel so good. So tight.'

And then, a memory: a traffic jam, gridlock, and the driver of a taxi asking me if I was into men, and telling me to hop up front. 'Here, next to me,' he says. 'Come on.' I'm terrified and turned on at the same time. As my foot touches the ground outside I wondered whether I should run or get back into the taxi, next to him. I open the door and sit down. And the man, at least a couple of decades older than me, and hairy – with black bristles poking out of his shirt and right up to his neck and the top of his back – pounces on me and kisses me. I pull away. 'First time?' he asks. I don't answer. 'You smell like a girl.' He turns into a side road, muttering something about the traffic. We come to a kind of scrubland. 'He's going to kill me,' I think. 'I don't want him to get angry.' The driver takes down his trousers. 'You like that?' he asks. It looks foul. And yet I say, 'Mmm.' He grabs me by the neck and pushes me down onto his cock. 'Open up,' he says, 'open up'. I open my mouth and… it's dirty and tastes of pee. 'No more,' I say. 'It's my first time.'

He smiles. 'Let me see you.' I pull my shirt up and my

trousers down. He moves in closer.

'That's how I like my boys, smooth-chested.' His tone changes and I smile, convinced now that he isn't going to kill me. He starts to touch himself, gets excited, then aggressive again.

'Come here.'

Frightened, I do as he says, and he comes on my face.

'It looks like tears,' he says, still smiling.

★ ★ ★

Dick. Click. Dick.

Sometimes I mistake my screen for the stranger's. I see myself masturbating and I think, 'But I'm not masturbating.' I ask myself, too: how many hours have I been on here?

★ ★ ★

Back in the corridor, I entered one of the rooms. A man, sprawled across the bed, erect and with his legs crossed, asked me to close the door. Older than me by twenty-odd years, he gave a little pat on the mattress to let me know I could join him.

I closed the door and sat on the bed. The man clasped me by the neck and rammed my face down onto his cock.

'Open,' he said, 'open'. Once again, I obeyed. 'Wider, no teeth.' And then, 'Make it nice and wet.'

He took my head in his hands and pulled me off his cock.

'Lie down,' he said, and I did, with my hands between the pillow and my head. He took out a condom and put it on. Next, he lifted up my legs and spat on my crack.

And then I felt a burning sensation, like veins bursting.

'Stop,' I said, and he didn't stop. 'Am I shitting?' I thought, before shouting, 'No, no, stop.' I pushed him.

'I said get off.' But the man, who was perfectly calm, seemed to think all I needed was more saliva.

'Easy,' he said, and he spat again. He also asked me to spit in his hand. I did and I felt some relief in my arse, but only for a matter of seconds. The burning came back. My veins still felt as if they were bursting, his cock a saw hacking away at my insides. My veins were like lightning rods.

* * *

Click. A man's body on another man's arm.

He has a beard and long hair, thorns all around his head. At the centre of his chest, a heart is on fire, with rays – lightning – bursting from the flames and shooting across the body of the man tattooed on the arm. The storm, in itself, forms a yellow star.

The stranger brings his arm up close to the camera.

'See him? Light of the world, let the light into your life.'

I click down.

I already knew about Jesus.

* * *

My feet were being held in the man's hands: when he opened his arms, he opened my legs, and all the while he was inside me. The burning turned to pain; and the pain to discomfort. I felt, basically, a straining sensation, the feeling of shitting without actually shitting. That's why I went on lying there, bored even, receiving the man patiently, as if a great invisible hand were pinning me against the bed.

He let go of my feet, then stroked and kissed my face.

'Is that good?' he asked.

'Yes,' I replied.

He kept kissing me: my eyes, my mouth. He kept moving: a mechanical in and out.

'Doesn't look like it,' he said.

I thought about sex faces. What kind was I pulling?

'Let's change position,' I said.

'Yeah, OK. Get on top,' he replied.

I got on top, facing him, and with a clearer idea of what he wanted, I began to perform: sitting on his stomach, I took his cock in my hand and slowly and steadily guided it inside me. Then came the faces: first, of suffering; frowning, as if realising, after a second, that what I was feeling was pain. I opened my mouth and formed ahs and ohs.

'It hurts,' I said, stifling moans.

Next, as I moved up and down, surprise: the look of not knowing what was going on. The expression to signal a change: it doesn't hurt anymore; I'm feeling something else now. I looked at him, saying 'That's it, give it to me,' riding him, 'Yeah, yeah,' saying 'You're making me so hot,' saying 'Kiss me.'

From those affirming, pleasing syllables, I moved on to pull my final face: the face of someone no longer thinking about their face. The gradual but resounding disappearance of any attempt at moderation. The face of being there without being there. I rolled my eyes back and opened my mouth wider. I groaned.

'It feels so deep,' I said, before planting my lips onto his.

And on hearing myself, it dawned on me that the man was, in fact, really deep, and I didn't have to act any more.

★ ★ ★

Some of us on Roulette are very polite.

'Please may I see your cock?' a stranger asks.

'Be my guest!' I reply, and tilt the camera down.

* * *

'That's enough,' I told the man, and I moved off him.

'You're gonna leave me like this?' he asked, agog.

'Like what?' I replied nonchalantly.

'Like this, without having come.'

'Well, yeah.'

* * *

Click. I want to come, and yet, what would I do then? Click, click. It unnerves me to be without *something*. Click. Something, in this very moment, is something to do.

Click.

* * *

In the corridor, a man was licking his lips. He looked at me and smiled; I smiled back, aloof, and he began to laugh. Then he covered his mouth. And he shuddered, as if receiving electric shocks, then jumped up and down with excitement.

The man held up one finger, the middle one, and with the other he made a circle. He raised his eyebrows and stuck the finger into the zero he'd formed. Then he pulled it out and put it back in again; as he repeated this, he pouted at me with his slobbering mouth.

Taken aback, I tried to ignore him, pretending I couldn't see. The man cried out, and even when I looked at him, clearly shocked, he went on shouting.

'Aaaaah, aaaah!'

And again.

'Aaaaah!'

He pointed to his own mouth and ears, and then he waved his hands as if to say 'No'.

'You can't hear? Can't speak?' I asked.

'Aaaaah, aaaah!' he replied, swinging his head around and around as he carried on drooling. I removed my towel.

'Come here,' I said, waving him over. The man leapt with joy. He let out a 'Oaaah, oaaah!' and walked towards me with his mouth wide open. There was dribble running down his chin.

I took his hand and put it on my cock. I looked at him and smiled.

'Fank youuu, paaal,' he said. 'Fank youuu.'

* * *

'I wanna show you something,' writes the stranger.

He lies down on a rug and looks into the camera, raising his thumb to check I'm still with him. For a couple of seconds he lies still, then he lifts up his legs. He makes an L shape with his body and stays like that for a while. Then he doubles over and stretches till his feet are grazing his head. He cranes his neck and sticks out his tongue – he's almost touching it. He keeps on trying. He masturbates. He's getting closer and closer to giving himself head. He gets tantalisingly close, but then lowers his legs and relaxes.

He tries again. And this time he manages to put a tiny bit of his cock in his mouth. He licks himself, sucks himself. And afterwards, he masturbates, pointing his cock at his face. Not long after, he comes.

The boy moves closer to the camera. He's flushed and out of breath. His face is splattered with white.

'Thanks,' I write.

* * *

I walked on and went through a door. And another. An old man called me into his room.

'Come in, take a seat,' he said, and then he held up a small glass bottle. 'Want some?'

I asked him what it was and he smiled.

'Take a huff,' he replied.

He unscrewed the top, held it up to his nose and breathed in deeply before inviting me to do the same.

The first thing I felt was my eyes almost rolling back on themselves. My mouth opened a little, too, as if in a lingering moan. I also felt the sudden urge to sit down. I did, on his bed, and my body sort of let go. That was the sensation. Woozy, I saw the old man take another sniff of the bottle.

'I'm going to go down on you,' I heard him say.

When he did, I felt everything a thousand times over: a thousand tongues blowing me, or a thousand dicks inside me, taken in one go.

I came. A bomb inside me. A thousand. More. And when I pulled out, away from his face, I didn't see a single drop of sperm. I asked him to open his mouth: there was still a little in there. I sucked his tongue, said bye and grabbed my towel.

* * *

Click. A macaw perched on the stranger's shoulder.

'Look,' he writes, standing up. He's naked, and the bird starts pecking the tip of his cock. I can see my own stupefied face on the screen. The stranger laughs and clicks down.

In the corridor, a boy, a redhead, called me over and got on all fours. When I reached him he handed me a condom.

'Put it in,' was all he said.

And when I did, nothing clasped me. A black hole engulfed my dick: that's how open he was.

I walked away, tossing the condom on the floor. A man was fucking another man in front of a mirror. They were standing up, and from certain angles it looked like there were four of them; even more so when the one being penetrated leant against the glass with his open hands: it looked like his hands were touching another man's, who was being penetrated as well.

The other one pulled his hair every now and then, and pushed his face against the glass.

'Kiss yourself,' he was saying. 'Kiss yourself.' And the man, obedient, kissed the mirror with his eyes closed.

★ ★ ★

Click. There are no strangers on the screen. Click. Click. Is there something wrong with Roulette? Click. At last, an image: a man with his back to me at the far end of a bathroom.

He's hanged himself.

Slowly but surely the body spins around to face me: I'm surprised, absurd as it sounds, to see he has a beard.

★ ★ ★

I was back, accidentally, in the red room.

The old man was still on the swing. When he saw I wasn't about to approach him, he checked the time and got off. He shuffled across the room looking down at his feet and closed the door carefully, so as not to make a sound.

★ ★ ★

'If you were here, with me,' writes the stranger, some years younger than me, 'I'd tie you to the bed'.

I ignore the message and keep on wanking. The kid, however, writes again.

'Stop. If you don't stop, I'm going to click down.'

I stop automatically, and then, a memory: the swing in Steam, the orders.

'Quick, find a shoelace,' the stranger writes.

I bend over and untie my shoe, feeling excited about what might happen. I hold the lace up to the camera and the man writes, 'Good, now tie your balls. Nice and tight. It's really got to hurt.'

'If you won't show your face, forget it.'

Silence.

'If you talk to me like that again, I'm clicking down.'

I do as he says again before he can act on his threat. For a second, it occurs to me that I could just not tie it very tightly, but in the end I decide to do exactly as he tells me. That obedience helps me imagine that we're in the same room.

I tie a noose around my balls with the lace. I pull, and it becomes a knot. Each time I do a new knot, the skin on my cock pulls back. Six, seven knots, I tie, eight, and then it feels like the skin can't stretch any more: another one and my frenulum will snap. My balls, meanwhile, and the head, start to turn purple.

'Good,' the kid says. 'Now move away from the camera and lean against the wall.'

I follow his instructions as I read the messages.

'Sit on one hand, either one, and toss yourself off with the other one.'

When I do as he says, my cock starts to hurt: the skin won't move and it burns. I want to untie the shoelace.

'Don't even think about removing the lace... Now smack your balls.'

'Smack them how?' I ask.

'With your hand.'

So I smack myself – my balls are even more puce now, and shiny – and I yelp.

'Do it again,' he says.

I let out another cry and catch sight of myself on the screen, in agony, and the image revives me. Without him even asking this time, I smack myself again. The screen transmits my pain.

'Now wet it, go on,' the stranger writes. 'Spit on it, I wanna see it nice and wet.'

It's a relief to feel the warm spit on my battered cock. Barely does the first dribble touch it and I rub it all over – across the head, down the veins – with my fingers. I read what he's written in capital letters:

'I DIDN'T TELL YOU TO TOUCH YOURSELF. JUST TO SPIT.'

But each time I do, I feel such relief – a liquid caress. I look at the screen: we're both biting our lips. He's started to masturbate.

'Do you want to do what I'm doing?' he asks.

'Yes.' And in a second message I add, 'Please.'

He tells me I can untie the lace.

'Thank you,' I type. With each knot that I undo, I feel both pleasure and gratitude.

'How do you feel?' he asks.

'Good,' I reply.

The kid smiles.

'Are you ready to come?'

'I've been ready for hours.'

He smiles again.

'Make yourself even wetter.'

I do as he says, convinced that only pleasure awaits me.

'Wet it, wet it,' he repeats. 'Make it really wet.'

Tired of spitting, finally, I watch another message appear.

'Good, now touch yourself.'

I start to wank and – oh, my body. My whole body becomes what I'm feeling in my cock.

'Are you close?' he asks.

'Yeah, really close.'

He smiles again. Silence. And then he says, 'Stop.'

'Why?'

'I want to see you in your underwear.'

'Let me finish and then I'll put them on,' I type, frustrated.

'No,' comes his reply.

I look for them, irritated, and then put them on in front of the camera.

He smiles again.

'That's enough for today,' and he clicks down.

★ ★ ★

In the red room, close to the swing, a man struck up a conversation with me. Apart from us it was still empty. He asked me what I was doing in there.

'I don't get why there are people in all the other rooms but not in this one.'

The man laughed – one chipped tooth – and slid an arm around my shoulder. He told me no one would go in as long as the old man was still on the swing.

'Good riddance to him, then,' I said, and immediately

regretted it, because I didn't really feel that way.

The man looked at me, smiled again, this time without baring his teeth, and ran one finger down my chest: he drew it lower and lower until he stopped at my belly button. I looked at him then. He had a thick beard, and tattooed on his arms were the words: *Love* and *God*.

'Want a go?' he said, gesturing to the swing.

'Sure,' I replied, and then, straight afterwards, there was that something, *something*: the tingling in my cock, the throbbing. I removed my towel, letting it fall to the floor. The man put one hand on my arse. He stroked it as we walked. He slipped his finger in.

'Hop on,' he said.

Someone poked their head around the door then came in and leant again the wall.

I lay down on my front, in suspense, suspended by the leather. The man pulled some chains and I rose into the air so that my head reached the exact height of his prick.

'Perfect,' he said, and when we kissed, his stubble scratched me. More men wandered in and surrounded us.

'It's best if you hold onto the sides,' he said.

I did as he told me, holding onto the chains tightly, clinging to them almost. The man held out a little bottle to me before unscrewing the top and huffing the contents. His mouth began to open.

'Ooh, that's nice. That's so good,' he said, rubbing his eyes.

'Put a condom on,' I said.

He inhaled some more. Then he passed it to me.

'Don't you worry about that,' he said.

I inhaled and instantly relaxed. The man took off his towel. I opened my legs even wider, and closed my eyes.

The cock slid in and kept on going, head and shaft. 'Ah.' It reached the very back, stayed there for a few seconds, then drew away. Once out, it went straight back in. 'Ah.' He gyrated in circles inside me. He pulled out, then slid back in. 'Ah.' I opened my eyes: more men all around, more eyes. I closed mine again. 'Ah, ah.' I felt the bottle nearby. The glass grazed my nose: I inhaled. A thousand dicks entered me. I inhaled again. A thousand more. 'Ah, ah.' A thousand hands all over my chest. A thousand-mouthed kiss. And oh, the cocks: once inside, there they remained. 'Ah, ah, ah.'

I opened my eyes. Four men were touching me: the bearded guy, who was screwing me; two more – two boys – licking my armpits; and the last one, who was kissing my face (he was so close I couldn't make him out). 'Ah, ah.'

The bottle again. I inhaled, closed my eyes. A sound: metal against the floor. And the men responding, 'Oh yeah.' Then something – *something* – in my mouth. I opened my eyes and… 'Ah. . .' I was sucking a cock. The boys had gone. I closed my eyes. 'Ah, ah.' And the cries, 'Do it, do it harder.' And then, emptiness: I could no longer feel those thousand cocks. I opened my eyes: the bearded man had gone. He'd made way for another, a young guy now, and as he entered me I yelped.

'You like 'em thick, don't you?' he asked, and there again, waved in front of my nose, was the bottle. I inhaled, I let myself go, and then some more. A thousand dicks, all thick, entered me now, one after the other… there was no end to them.

I opened my eyes. Another man's cock was in my mouth. It was a different colour, and it was bent. I closed my eyes again. 'Let me have a go,' someone said. In my mouth, in my arse, the pricks kept arriving, more and more as time went on.

I opened my eyes again. Another man – hairy, he had hairy shoulders – was fucking me. A cock slid out of my mouth. I turned my head. I needed a break. Another was rammed in. I closed my eyes, and again, there was the smell of the bottle. I inhaled, and, lying down, I rolled from side to side. I felt emptiness, emptinesses. I opened my eyes and... I was pulling away from the man in my arse. For a moment, I saw him from far off, from up in the air. Then I flew back down. He thrust it in again – a thousand cocks, a thousand. 'Ah, ah.' I drew up and away, and then back down. In mid-air I realised I was swinging.

When I flew back down towards the man, he stopped the swing, wanked me off for a minute, then left. Another arrived. I could see a queue. I closed my eyes and heard laughter. 'Open wider.' The thousand cocks entered me again, and a thousand mouths kissed and sucked me as they did. 'Don't let him come,' one of them said. 'Keep him here.' And another, 'The bottle, the bottle.' I opened my eyes – another cock in my mouth – and suddenly, in the queue, I spotted a familiar face. The men kept pushing the swing and I swung back and forth. A cock went in. 'Ah, ah.' Out. And in my head I kept thinking about the man I'd spotted in the queue. 'I know him. I know that man.'

'My turn,' another said. In, out. 'Ah, ah.'

'Who is he?' I thought. 'Who is he?' and 'Ah, ah.' Another. 'Ah, ah.' And in my mouth, another dick. 'Who is he? Who is he?' And, 'Hard. Give it to him harder.' A kiss. A thousand. 'Ah, ah.' And then, 'I know, I know.'

There was still a line, and the next man came forward. 'Ah, ah.' I tried to speak, but I couldn't. 'It's him,' I thought. 'It's him.' And I said 'Mm, mm.' I couldn't. I spat him out. One of them said, 'He wants more cock.' I spat. 'He loves sucking cock.' And I said, 'Mm, mm,' even though in my head I was saying, 'No, no.' And then, more cocks. 'Ah, ah.' The man in the queue was coming towards me. I wanted to say, 'No, not him,' but instead I said, 'Mm, mm'.

And the others, meanwhile, said, 'The bottle, the bottle.'
And without wanting to, I inhaled. And in my head, 'Not
him, not him.' He was getting closer. Another went in,
another drew out. A thousand dicks. 'Ah, ah.' The next
one in line was the man I recognised. 'Mm, mm.' And I
heard someone say, 'Look! Look, he's lapping it up!' And
when I tried to jump off they said 'Look at him riding
that thing!'

I began to wriggle more. I still had a cock in each
of my hands, but I let them go. And I spat, and as I did,
a cock spilt out of my mouth. 'Easy boy,' one of them
said. 'What's up with you?' And I said, 'Mm, mm,' but
then, finally, 'Not him, not him.' So much saliva! Then
someone asked me, 'Which one?' and I said, 'Him, him.'

I shook them off and hopped down from the swing.
My legs lurched. The others all stepped back, making way
for me. I shouted at the man, the one I'd seen outside, on
the street.

'Don't you touch me! You were laughing at me.'

* * *

Sometimes, when I'm on Roulette chatting to torsos,
I start picturing both the most beautiful and the most
deformed faces. Faces with a hand coming out of
a cheek, for example; a little hand that pops out of a
hollow, waves, and then retreats again. Both kinds turn
me on: I think about the beautiful ones watching me
on the screen, becoming deformed with excitement, or
becoming more beautiful still. And then the same with
the ugly ones: their mouths and eyes open as they see
me; they become even more deformed, or as pretty as a
picture.

I click down and the screens freeze: for a second, the
body and I are stuck there. I hear a beep, beep, beep and

the connection fails. I move the computer around, trying to reconnect. Nothing. The screen is back working now, but there's still no signal to write. I'm starting to worry about what may await me: hours without Roulette, which will only intensify the boredom. I glance at myself on the screen. I look anxious. Seconds later, I'm someone else entirely.

I shut down the computer and shut myself off, folding over in hunger. I think 'What if I sell it and tell Ramón-Ramona it got stolen?' I look at the screen, which is now black, and start to feel restless. I turn it back on. I think about my dad and get up to go to his room, where I stare at him – and as I do, I think about him. I think about myself, too.

★ ★ ★

I couldn't find my towel when I got off the swing.

'That's enough,' I told one of the men, who tried to touch me. 'Fun's over, get out.' And no sooner had I said those words than the crowd began to disperse.

I could hardly stand at first, and it was the same when I tried to walk. Feeling light-headed, I made for the showers, shuffling along slowly so as not to fall. I stood for a while under the water, holding on to the taps, waiting to regain my balance.

When I finally did, I turned off the taps and went out to the locker room, wondering what to do. I took out the other towel and dried myself. I saw the exit, facing away from the labyrinth, and then, inside, the three doors. Although tempted to go back down one of the corridors, I opted to put on my costume and head out into the street. I walked away from the sea, in the direction of my dad: in the direction of the place that would soon no longer be my home.

★ ★ ★

When I think about who I am, I think about the night I dressed up as a butterfly. Three things happened that night, in succession and totally unforeseen. Three transformations, which I immediately recognised as both monumental and definitive. First, I discovered I was a poor man, with the news my dad gave me. Second, I discovered infinity, which is not the same as excess or repetition, by entering the labyrinth and going on the swing. And third, I became a father to my father when I stepped into our flat to find him sitting on a chair, neither speaking nor moving. Unable to speak or move.

Despite these events, which even now I understand as monumental and definitive, one memory of that night supplants all others: the vision of the old man on the swing, open and nude, looking at his watch. I've thought a lot about the sadness of a man who offers himself up, who wants to give himself to others only to be ignored and rejected. The spectacle without an audience, the birthday party without guests. Something about that memory that leaves me particularly shaken: his patience on the swing as he kept checking the time. How long must he have spent there, suspended in flight, suspended in his desire?

I invented one memory from that night, and now I can't remember if I made it up on the spur of the moment, or if I've fabricated it slowly over time. In this memory I bump into the old man after getting off the swing. He fiddles with his towel – doing it up then undoing it, over and again – and asks me if I'm OK. And I tell him I am, but that I regret inhaling so much from the bottle.

'The dizziness does go away, don't worry,' he says. 'They had a real feast, eh?'

'I ate my fair share too,' I reply with a smile. Afterwards, while I'm making up my mind in the locker room whether to stay or go, the old man appears again. He invites me to his room, tells me it's a double. And in my memory, then, I debate whether or not to go with him. I look at him and try to imagine him without the towel, me on top of him, him on top of me, and, feeling disgusted, I force myself to think about something else. 'No, thanks,' I say, to which he responds, impulsively, grabbing me by the wrist, 'Please, son.' I shrug him off and explain that I've spent too long in there, that I want to get out. The old man insists, 'What's another hour...' but I dismiss him with a wave of my hand.

I'm surprised at myself, and disappointed, that not even in that memory am I capable of fucking him. Not even in the knowledge of his wait there on the swing, his frustrated desire. It changes nothing. Having witnessed his patience – and thinking about his patience – makes me lose sight of his desire. Thinking about his desire only heightens my aversion. That aversion is my failure.

* * *

'What's wrong?' I asked my dad back inside the flat. 'Why aren't you talking? What's wrong?' I turn on more lights, and take off my boots and costume wings.

'Can you hear me? Say something.'

Silence.

'Pa? I'm back. Come on, let's talk.' I went up to him and blew on his face, but he just sighed and closed his eyes.

'We'll find a place to live. Don't worry about that,' I said.

Silence.

And again, 'I've actually been thinking, and what's the big deal about moving anyway? It's nothing. We'll still be together.'

Just then, a photo appears projected onto the wall. A photo of us together: me in my dad's arms, crying, while he looks at me and points to the camera, trying to get me to smile.

'Look at the photo, Pa. What a crybaby I was, eh?'

Silence.

I resorted to platitudes.

'Every cloud. It'll be alright in the end. Everything happens for a reason.'

He glanced at me and then closed his eyes again. I looked for the telephone. With each number I dialled, I became more terrified by what was happening.

'Yes, good evening,' I said. 'I'd like to report an emergency.' The man asked me a series of questions, which I answered. 'My dad has stopped speaking. He's not moving or talking. I don't know what's happening. He's stopped talking.'

'Hang up,' came Pa's voice from behind me. 'There's no money for that.'

* * *

The signal's back. I open Roulette, more than a little indifferently. When a torso appears, I click the arrow down. Click. Click. An old man waves at me.

'Hey,' he writes. 'What are you looking for?'

'You,' I reply, and I blow him a kiss.

CHAPTER IV

Getting Lost

There were boxes all over the floor, and items of clothing strewn among them. I picked up one at random, a white vest with holes in it.

'Do you want to take this?' I asked my dad, just to coax him into saying something, to involve him in the house move.

He sized up the vest from his spot on the sofa, then nodded listlessly — vacantly — and closed his eyes. A second later, he started snoring.

'It has some sweat stains,' I said, very loudly, to wake him up, 'but aside from that it looks unworn.' But my dad slept on (or pretended to).

He was in better spirits now, or at least that's the impression I got. Before then, he hadn't left his bed for nights, hadn't said a word, hadn't moved, unless I went over to try and tease a smile from him with a term of endearment ('Love, love, love,' I'd say, kissing his forehead and cheeks) or a joke. Then he might raise his finger, or thumb, as if to say he was OK (or would be) before turning on his side, away from me. Eventually he started walking again, from the bedroom to the sofa, and now and then he'd pick up some piece of detritus from the floor. He would also scan the classified ads for second-hand furniture.

We started packing before we even found a place to move into. The first thing we did – the first thing I did – was to close the shop. We'd opened it some time ago, a few blocks away, in a poorly lit area, and shared the running of it between us. It was called Nibbles and we only opened at night, since my dad didn't want to steal – that's the word he used – hard-won customers from neighbouring shops. 'Friends, not competitors'.

'We'll find our own customers before long,' he'd say. 'They'll be loyal to the shop, and we'll be loyal to them.'

We sold tuna, rice, jam… Products with expiry dates that seemed a long way away. Biscuits, beans…

'We can't sell milk or vegetables,' he explained. 'Not for the time being. They might spoil before anyone comes to buy them.' And so, when someone asked if we had celery, or tomatoes, we'd reply in unison, 'Why not take this tasty tuna instead?' Some people followed our advice and bought two or three cans. Others threw the offer in our faces.

'You never have anything!' they'd yell, storming out the door without so much as saying goodnight.

During his shifts at the shop, my dad would write lists of all the products customers asked for that we didn't sell – and that had a long shelf life, like liquor and medicine. He'd crunch some numbers and come to depressing conclusions.

'We can't sell that, there's not enough money in it.'

To cheer himself up, he recalled his favourite inspirational phrases – 'You've got to be in it to win it' – before running us into debt buying boxes of candles, condoms, coat hangers. Often the people who'd requested a specific product never came back and my dad would be left high and dry, unable to let them know that we now stocked their item.

Drunks would come in, too, in droves, all the time.

They'd ask for soup, or anything to help them sober up.

'Look, a pitstop,' I heard a guy tell his chum one night, before staggering into Nibbles. 'Hungry, hungry,' he grunted, and let out a burp.

Pa would give the drunks tuna, and although most of the time they ate it without complaint, it wasn't unusual for one of them to kick the counter or walls, yelling that he wanted a bowl of fresh soup and was sick to death of those tins.

'There aren't even any tables in this shithole!' they'd grumble.

If they got violent we chased them out with a broom, or dragged them out by the hair, saying, 'Go and yell at someone else, arsehole.' And from the door I'd warn the others, 'Anyone gets rowdy, they're out.' Some customers applauded this, praising my tough, no-nonsense attitude. Others complained about me to my dad, saying I was extremely rude and nothing like him. My dad would look at them, then at me, and not say a word.

I thought about the drunks and the shop – and about my dad in the shop, and all his plans to expand the business – as I sealed our boxes with packing tape. Lots of them were still full of unsold stock from Nibbles – rice and beans, mostly, and toothpaste – and although I was disappointed we still had so much unsold merchandise, I took comfort in knowing we had food (and other products) to last a while.

'They're nearly done, the boxes,' I said to my dad. 'Have you found any apartments?' From the bed, and without looking at me, he handed me the newspaper: he'd circled possible housing options with a crayon. I checked and almost all of them were over budget. There was one house available, though, with two bedrooms and a big living room. I was terrified of the location, right in the heart of the dark zone – as it was called – which had no street lights at all, but the price was within what we could afford. I made some calls, I talked it over with my dad. A couple of evenings later we visited the neighbourhood, wandered around and viewed the house. Although we weren't entirely convinced, we decided to take it. Immediately, we focused on the positives.

'It's not that far from our old place,' we said. 'We'll miss the light, but now we'll have the sea for a neighbour.'

★ ★ ★

My dad is out of bed again. And he's speaking, saying the odd thing.

'What do you get up to on that computer all the time?' he asks at precisely the moment the actor I'm following, and who looks like me (so much like me), opens a jar of honey and sticks his fingers in before calmly wanking off with his honeyed hand. I turn the volume down.

'Nothing much, Pa. Just browsing where to buy food.' It's partly true: I've been checking our pantry every night.

'You're going out?' he asks, padding over to my bedroom door. 'It's dangerous.'

Meanwhile, in the video, a beefy man wearing shades and all black enters the room and walks up to the first guy (me), pointing and gesticulating. He (I) appears to follow his orders: he pours honey on himself, and, facing the camera, spreads it all over his chest. He drenches his hairy armpits in sweetness.

'Don't worry, I won't be long.'

'Don't give me that,' and my dad looks up at the ceiling. 'It's dangerous.'

The empty jar appears on the screen, then a shot of his cock, dripping with honey.

'Don't worry. It's safe around the shops up the hill, towards town.'

'Dangerous,' my dad insists.

The man in black smiles. He's acting pleased, as if he's got *something* out of it. The camera then focuses on my double, his hands and legs tied to a table: his (our) body forms an X.

'Don't go out, we can eat later.'

The camera slides over us, just like the honey. Someone – perhaps the lighting technician or the cameraman – hands a new jar to the man in shades. He smiles as opens it and studies the contents. My double moans and squirms, at which point we get a close-up of the container: inside it's teeming with black ants.

'I'm just popping out, you stay right here. Don't worry, I won't be long,' I say.

'Do you have to walk past the bodies?'

The jar is tipped over his chest – his, mine. The ants come pouring out and make for the sweetness, and I, no, he, still on mute, starts screaming.

★ ★ ★

The van we hired arrives at last, hours later than agreed.

'Don't expect punctuality, with the pittance you're paying me,' said the driver, without so much as a hello. He glanced at the boxes and sighed. Trying to rein in his irritation, he spoke through gritted teeth.

'You're going to have to help me carry those. I'm not doing it all on my own.'

'Of course we will, pal,' my dad replied. 'Six hands make light work, lighter than two.'

I was surprised to hear Pa's enthusiasm. I hugged him and gave him a kiss, to celebrate his gradual return to his old self. Equally enthused, I picked up a box and put it on my shoulder.

'All hands on deck,' I said, to which Pa replied,

sounding even more chipper, 'All hands on deck.' Addressing the driver, he added, 'You, you're younger, grab those big boxes over there. I'll take care of these ones.'

A few things got broken along the way: a coffee table, the slide projector. When we reached the neighbourhood, my dad decided we should pull over so he could ask the first passer-by for directions.

'But I know the way,' the driver snapped. 'I don't need directing.'

'That's not the point, my friend. Come on, let's get to know the neighbours.'

So we stopped at the next block by a vendor cart, which was painted in green letters, 'Coconuts and chewing gum'. It was attended by an old woman. Her face was dirty and when she saw us she said, 'I'm out of coconuts, and if you want chewing gum, I've only got peppermint.' My dad popped his head out of the window.

'How do you do, madam? What a lovely evening.'

'I've got peppermint,' the woman yelled back, hands on hips. 'How many do you want?'

'Which way is Lights Avenue?' I interrupted, trying to stick to my dad's original plan.

'Ach, that's all the way down there,' and she waved her hands as if to push the street away from her. 'Down the hill, right in the lion's den.'

The driver pulled away, letting us know he wasn't prepared to waste his time. He reiterated that we weren't paying him enough to make stops along the way.

'It's alright, pal,' my dad said. 'Take some deep breaths.'

The man curled his lip.

When we got to the house, we noticed the van's exhaust pipe was hanging half-off.

'For fuck's sake,' said the driver, 'why didn't you tell me there were this many boxes to be moved?' He scratched his head and spat on the floor. 'My own bloody fault for agreeing to take you.'

'It's alright,' my dad repeated, and then he asked the driver to give us a moment. He called me over, and we did some calculations.

'Sir,' we said in the end, 'we wish we could give you more money, but the truth is we don't have much more. Take this, for your troubles.'

Seeing the man's face, red with rage at the paltry amount, it occurred to me to tell him about our leftover stock.

'If you wait for us to open the boxes, we can give you a few tins of tuna. And toothpaste, we've got quite a few tubes.'

He called me a son of a bitch, got into the van and drove off, the exhaust pipe clattering all the way down the road.

* * *

'Don't worry,' I repeat to my dad, and then again, this time from the pavement, 'Don't worry.' I come back to the door, give him a hug and a kiss. I tell him again that some nights ago, when he went out for bread, he got back home without running into any trouble. 'Yes, son,' he says, 'but there were people around. There's no one left now.'

I kiss him – another kiss – and turn to walk away. And this time I keep walking – as always, following an imaginary straight line – relieved, even, to be out of the house, sadly grateful for the excuse, afforded by hunger, to go out. 'There's no food,' I repeat aloud to myself. 'There's no food, but I'll find some.'

On reaching the street corner I'm tempted to take a detour to the bar district. I do it. There seems to be some light coming from the next block. I hear noises too, people talking, and I head in that direction. There's an area cordoned off with yellow tape. 'Danger', 'Do not cross'. I crane my neck to get a better look, but my gaze is met by a policeman, who peers back at me.

'Are you taking the bodies away?' I ask.

'Freeze,' he yells, striding towards me. 'What do you think you're doing?'

'I live nearby.'

'Freeze,' he repeats.

I put my hands above my head to placate him.

'I live nearby, like I said, right there,' and I point at our unlit street. 'I came out looking for some food.'

Another policeman approaches. He's wearing a mask and he asks me the same question.

'He says he lives nearby,' the first one answers for me.

Feeling calmer now, I lower my hands.

'Easy, easy,' one of the policemen says, and I raise them again.

They order me to turn around. I do as they say. Then they search me.

'What's this?' I hear when they discover the cardboard star. 'A necklace,' they answer their own question and burst out laughing.

The first policeman grabs me by the chin and scrutinises me, leaning right in towards my face with his own. Utterly disinterested, he says to the other policeman, or to no one, 'How come they didn't kill this one, though?'

A momentary silence.

Then, more laughter.

* * *

We'd only just moved in when we met Olguita, who dropped by the house to introduce herself and offer us a hand with anything we needed, as she put it, before handing Pa some cakes.

'Why, thank you, neighbour,' he said. 'You shouldn't have.'

Olguita slipped off one of her sandals and smacked it against the wall to swat an insect.

'I didn't make them,' she said, flustered. 'They're from the shop.'

'But come in, come in,' my dad said. 'I'll get you a glass of water.'

'That would be nice, thanks. I need to take my tablet.'

Olguita opened her sequined bag, pulled out a tattered white carrier bag, and dumped its contents onto our table: loose pills and little sachets of medicine.

'Let's see which one is calling me,' she mused, and after a moment's indecision, she picked one at random. 'Oh, these aches and pains, I can't tell you...'

I asked her what the matter was.

'I don't even know anymore,' Olguita replied, before knocking back the pink pill. And as I put the cakes away in the cupboard, I heard her say, as if responding to the drug in her body, 'Oh goodie, I love this one.'

We saw Olguita every evening. Sometimes she came over to ours, and sometimes we went to hers. We'd take three rocking chairs out onto the pavement, sit and have a 'good old chinwag' – as Olguita liked to say. A chinwag, in practice, meant us replying to her questions and then turning them back on her so she spoke as well. That's how we got to know each other: chatting about the shop and the flat where we used to live, back in our old neighbourhood where there were more street lights. Olguita would reel off her ailments and her favourite tablets for treating them, each one stronger than the last. We also spoke, a lot, about our own burdens.

'I think they're going to cut off our electricity,' I said one night.

'It'll be fine,' Olguita replied matter-of-factly. I wasn't sure if that helped or made me more anxious.

'If they cut it off, you can reconnect it yourselves. I'll show you how. Just be sure never to switch on a light you can see from the street.'

'Why not, Olguita?'

'So those crooks from the electricity board don't find out about the reconnection, stupid.'

We could laugh with Olguita, and at her, too. We enjoyed her company. One night, though, on noticing that my dad was down in the dumps, or a bit vacant perhaps, Olguita popped a tablet, called my dad 'brother' and started counselling him.

'I know where your head's at. It's out there, on that grimy street where you live now, you and your son. Listen, don't go getting bogged down by dark thoughts. I want you to know there's a man you can count on. His name is Jesus, and he came to my door one night when I was in the most unimaginable pain.'

Pa and I looked at her, surprised by this new Olguita, feeling that we were just getting to know her.

'You may have heard about him, about where he came from, perhaps. That he's the son of God and a virgin, Mary, and that he was born in a manger surrounded by animals. You probably know how the animals gobbled up his umbilical cord, ravenous they were, and how they bathed him in saliva, and gave him warmth – and that gentle warmth made great waters boil. You'll have heard that he grew up to preach about love, and that, as he made his way around the world, he promised more life – an eternal life, after this one, in another realm entirely. You'll have heard all about how he ran right across the sea without treading on a single fish; just startling them. You know about his outrage over the famines, and how he turned all the hair those desperate, starved men and women were tearing out into wheat. You've probably heard that when he died he didn't die. Quite the opposite: by dying without dying he gave us life. But that's not the full story: he didn't die, he was murdered, and that's the truth. Dying and being murdered are not the same thing, and it's important to know the difference. Some people say he was never even born, but let me tell you he's born in me every single night. My encounters with Jesus are his unknown history.'

'He lives with me. Within me, and outside of me. When he's inside me, I feel electrified, like when you go to a place with high ceilings and you hear music and it's night-time and your arms just rise into the air of their own accord and then something – *something* – happens inside you: a trembling that builds and builds and shakes you apart before putting you back together. It's the breeze that moves you without actually moving you, and without even being a breeze.'

'Jesus also leaves my body sometimes. Not to actually leave me, but to be by my side. When I look at him, time begins to stall. Jesus is time. He's the son of God but he *is* God, his own son and his own dad, ancestors and descendants, line and circle. And I swear to you, brother, that when he sits here, in this rocking chair, and when I stare at him, I see origins and endings. In his face I can see time: his crown of thorns, and the spikes of a stegosaurus. I see him at all different ages – elderly, teenage and newborn – speaking to God, speaking to himself. He says, "Father, why have you forsaken me?" He says, "Olguita, I like your hair," or, "Boo, boo, wah, wah," like the whining babe he once was. He also tells me, "Love yourself in this way, as I love you." All of this simultaneously. Jesus is time.'

Olguita sighed and popped another pill, a blue one – hoping, she said, that the effect would last this time.

'It hurts here and here,' she groaned, touching her back and legs, seemingly at random. 'One night,' she continued, 'I was in agony. I thought I might sink into a coma. I was losing my mind. But suddenly Jesus arose; he was born in my body. He spoke to me, looked at me. I saw sparks. I saw myself newly born and our planet, too, being born – first the dust and then gravity, then the dust turning to rock, and the rock to molten lava, bubbling away, slowly becoming the world we live in. Jesus said to me: "Be well now," and I was well again. Then I saw his thirty-three years and the thirty-three million light years that separate us from a planet that's like this one, only twenty times bigger. On it I saw thousands of men and women with squat legs and long torsos. I saw them tied to the branch of a tree, and then standing up straight, walking. Jesus said, "Let's go to the sea," and we went to the sea. When we got there, I asked him to do me a favour. I asked him not to walk on the water because it sets my nerves on edge. Jesus did as I asked and stayed put on the sand.'

'Every time the pain comes back, Jesus does just that: he's born in me. He takes me to the sea, I take him to the city. And we walk past my old house and I grow melancholy remembering all my dearly departed, so Jesus hugs me and says, "You will see them again." I don't know if I believe him, and he knows that and he doesn't mind. Despite my lack of faith, he keeps coming back. He eases my yearning.'

My dad's eyes filled with tears as Olguita spoke. I looked at him, and looked at the sky and the pills and my dad looking at her, not quite knowing what to think. Perhaps seeing me like this triggered a memory in Olguita, because all of a sudden she became quite agitated.

'People have called me mad. People say my story makes them uncomfortable, that I'm addicted to pain and that it's Jesus's fault, because he promised more life to those who suffer. I've been called poor by people who are richer than me: poor because, instead of keeping on working through all my aches and pains, I've stayed at home, thinking up ways – be it Jesus, a cure, *something* – to make the pain go away. And which shows greater resignation: going to work tormented by pain, or devoting yourself to getting better? Those people have more money than me, and they look down on me for precisely that reason. They say I'm in love with misery. But they're wrong, brother: my life hasn't been misery alone. There's also been joy, and lots of it, and all those people spouting opinions will never understand it. So I'm telling you: if you feel like crying, then cry. And think about Jesus. Think about his promises: I've never cared whether he keeps them or not. I've never kept mine.'

Olguita got up from the rocking chair, cracked her back and let out a whimper. Then she closed her eyes, waiting, she said, for Jesus to be born.

'Whenever he's born and he comes out and stands beside me, I just stare at him, deeply in love. Sometimes, when I see him, I see it all: a mass, a shift in temperature and a boundless violence: the beginning appears, the big bang. Jesus has told me he's seen it too, once or twice, when he looks at his reflection on the water. And yet, sometimes, like now, he won't be born out of me and I can't feel or see him. That doesn't worry me, though. Jesus has told me that sometimes his reflection doesn't appear in the water because sometimes there's just nothing. He's also nothing.'

★ ★ ★

With their laughter, my hatred grows.

'How come they didn't kill this one?'

When I feel this level of hatred, I'm eradicated and magnified at once. First I feel the violence done to me erasing my whole past and any future. All that exists is the present, and the present is nothing but that violence. Because the past is erased, everything the past did to me vanishes with it. I empty out, and all the hatred directed at me turns into the hatred that I am. I'm amplified: I desire bad things, I want to kill, and I feel capable of killing.

'How come they didn't kill this one?'

I want to kill them.

★ ★ ★

Out one night with Olguita, strolling from her house to ours and from ours to hers – a circuit we did when we'd had enough of the rocking chairs or when we decided we needed a change of scene – we ran into the coconuts and chewing gum lady. She was pushing her cart, complaining, it seemed, about the heat and the very fact of having to lug the stall around. We saw her stop and say, 'Oh, no, no, no. I'm too old for this,' fanning her face with her skirt. As soon as she spotted us, though, she stood up straight and called out.

'Come and get your juicy green mangos, mangos and salt. I've got sweets, too: strawberry and watermelon.'

'Hey, Yadira!' Olguita called out. 'What are you doing dragging that great big contraption around?'

'I'm heading over to The Letcher, where it's busier. Won't you buy something?'

'Oh, sweetheart, if only I could,' Olguita said. She was pensive for a while, then added, 'Let's all head to The Letcher, these two will help you with the cart.'

So we went to the bar. The women talked about their evening and about life in general, saying over and over how sad and difficult it was. My dad and I pushed the cart while crunching numbers, deciding how much we could spend.

'I think we can afford to have one beer each,' Pa said. 'Olguita included.'

'A beer sounds nice,' Olguita said. 'It fills you up, that's the good thing: fills your belly with gas, stops you feeling hungry.'

On the opposite pavement, a drunk was trying to tie his shoelace.

'Did one of you just hug me?' he asked. Then he paused, waiting for an answer, and when he didn't get one, he kicked a bollard. 'Sons of bitches,' he yelled. 'Sons of bitches, every last one of you!'

When we reached the entrance to The Letcher, Yadira took back her cart. She thanked us curtly; I couldn't tell whether it was just her manner, or if our help made her feel uncomfortable. 'Have a nice time,' she added. My dad bought some sweets off her. 'Thank *you*,' he said, and we went in.

The first thing I saw was a naked woman, fully waxed, dancing on the stage. Below, standing between the tables, were men and women whistling and applauding. 'That girl there,' a lady said to me, pointing at the dancer with her cigarette, 'I waxed her pubic hair. She had quite a bush.'

Meanwhile, the girl twirled on the stage, wrapped herself around a pole, crawled towards the bar. At one point she sat on a stool to blow kisses at the audience.

'Mwah,' she said. 'Mwah.'

'I'd rather you blew me!' someone yelled, and everyone laughed.

The girl crossed her legs. I couldn't tell whether she was really offended or pretending to be, and you could hear hecklers.

'Boo, you look ugly like that!' a man yelled.

'Bad girl,' chimed another.

The girl spread her legs again.

'That's better!' a few of them cried, and the whole audience applauded.

I went over to my dad, who seemed uncomfortable.

'Are you alright?' I asked him.

'Yes, yes. Let's go and grab a beer.'

At the bar, we met the bartender.

'You two are new, welcome,' Ramón-Ramona said before turning away, taking someone else's order and yelling into the crowd, 'I'll charge you for the ice if you keep throwing it at people!'

'How much is the beer?' Pa asked.

'Three, five or seven, depending on which.'

Silence.

'And how much are the cocktails?'

'They're more expensive,' Ramón-Ramona said. 'Ten and twelve.'

My dad called me over. We did some calculations.

'We've got enough for three bottles of the three-dollar beer,' I told him.

'Alright, what's it gonna be then?'

'Just a second, please,' my dad said.

Ramón-Ramona continued serving the people around us.

'We won't have enough left to leave a tip. Don't you have anything?' said Pa. I checked my pockets, knowing I didn't, silently willing some coins to appear.

'Nothing,' I said.

'Then order one for yourself and another for Olguita.'

'No, no. I really don't want one.'

My dad took out the smaller note from his wallet and left it on the bar as a tip for Ramón-Ramona, who was busy mixing more drinks.

As we walked off to look for Olguita my dad tried to defend his decision to leave a tip. 'Well, we did dither for a long time, and he is such a nice bartender. Look how packed it is in here!'

⋆ ⋆ ⋆

All that exists is a policeman who's just asked another policeman a question: how come whoever killed the others didn't kill me. The only thing that exists is their laughter.

I don't recognise myself, reduced to this absolute present, and yet I also recognise myself fully: I've experienced this state a thousand times before. I've *been* violence, a thousand times. Hatred guides me to other places and times. I think back to the swing, my inability to speak, watching a man approaching who I want to stay far away; I think back to The Letcher, to the evening of the fight… I'm here, and there, and there… I'm many different people, all of them at once. Hate multiplies me.

'How come they didn't kill this one?' I'm going to kill them.

⋆ ⋆ ⋆

In the queue for the toilets women were standing with their backs to the door, watching what was happening onstage. Among them was Olguita, chatting to the people around her and sipping her beer. 'Oh, my girl,' I heard her say, 'if you think you had it hard pushing *one* out, imagine giving birth to Jesus every night.'

I walked over to them. I was going to tell Olguita we'd been looking for her, but she beat me to it.

'*This* is the guy I was telling you about,' she told them, putting one hand on my shoulder. There was a moment's silence, then she bobbed her head and added, 'And that's his father.' She pointed into the distance (throughout all this, my dad was drumming his fingers to a beat totally out of sync with the music).

'Your dad's so handsome,' the other woman said to me, shaking my hand. 'But tell me something, is he like you? I'm Leda.'

'How do you mean, "like me"?' I asked, confused.

'What kind of question is that?' Olguita butted in, and I couldn't tell if she was speaking to her or to me.

Next thing, everyone in the bar started clapping. On the stage, the same girl was strutting about with a bag of sweets.

'I hope she bought them off Yadira,' was what I thought.

'Me, me!' the crowd cried.

Some women abandoned the queue and ran towards the stage.

'Me!' they kept yelling. 'Me, Briseida, me!'

Briseida took a sweet from the bag, opened her legs, and popped it inside her, amid even more commotion.

'Me, please, me!'

Briseida smiled at her audience and, after a moment's hesitation, placed the moist sweetie between the lips of a man who'd been standing in front of the stage for a while with his mouth open expectantly.

'Nooo,' the crowd booed.

'There's more, there's more,' Briseida replied.

'Hooray!' they cried. 'Me, me!'

I turned away from Leda without saying goodbye, and told Olguita I was going to stand with my dad.

'Look at that,' she said, visibly angry and pointing at a drunk. 'Why does he have to be sick on the dancefloor when he knows full well there are toilets?' Just then, three women could be seen dragging the man across the floor. They leaned him against a column, railed at him for not being able to hold his drink, and then marched straight back to the dancefloor.

'*Bite me, scratch me,*' went the song overhead. '*Rip my clothes off.*'

I walked over to my dad, feeling about ready to get out of there.

'Shall we go?' I asked.

'No. Let's stay a little longer.' He started drumming his fingers again as if he were enjoying the music, encouraging me to do the same.

'Shove another one up there!' a woman said to Briseida. 'Give it to me!'

I heard a noise, like glass smashing, and then Ramón-Ramona asked, 'What's going on over there, eh?' A young woman stood up and held a broken bottle up to her neck – which, I supposed, was the one she had just smashed.

She was bellowing.

'If you all keep looking at Briseida, I'll kill myself.'

Silence. Then Ramón-Ramona spoke up:

'Carry on dancing, everyone, that's what you came here to do.'

There was a round of applause before Ramón-Ramona came out from behind the bar to talk to the girl.

'You need to learn to love yourself,' I overheard. 'You can't keep smashing bottles: you might get hurt. And the bar has to pay for them.' The young woman let go of the broken shard and said, 'But I want them to look at me, not just her.'

'Briseida!' they carried on yelling. 'Give me a sweetie!'

'Me too, me too! A wet one!'

My dad went over to the girl. I followed. She was still talking.

'When I go up the hill, up where all the lights are, and I see those billboards glowing with all the things I don't have, I ask myself whether nobody looks at me because I'm ugly, or because I don't look like that or have any of those things.'

'I've got two left,' Briseida announced. 'Who wants them, huh? Say "me".'

'Me!' rang through The Letcher. 'Me!'

Ramón-Ramona laughed, delighted by Briseida and the patrons' reaction, but then turned back and asked the young woman, 'Why would you give a damn about those drunks?'

'Sonofabitch!' someone yelled.

'Yer ma!'

'*Your* ma!'

More sounds of glass smashing.

I glimpsed Briseida handing the sweet to a woman, and an outraged man shoving her out of the way to grab it. The woman fell, then stood up and punched him.

'Don't be such a pushover!' someone cried, and I couldn't tell if they were talking to the man or the woman. The man shoved her again, and then another man pushed him, knocked him to the floor and kicked him.

'Leave him alone,' a woman interrupted, and hit the kicking man. The first woman gathered herself and continued fighting.

'Stop it, stop, please,' Briseida begged from up on the stage.

'It's her fault!' someone yelled, and threw a bottle at her.

'Sonofabitch!' someone else replied, and smashed a jug on his head.

'Fight!' the crowd yelled. 'Fight!' And the punching and shoving snowballed.

Ramón-Ramona ran onto the dancefloor.

'Sonofabitch!' people shouted. 'Sonofabitch!'

The chain of blows reached my dad: someone pushed him against a drunk, who then pushed my dad against a column.

'Sonofabitch, sonofabitch!'

I could feel myself emptying out. I could feel that the only thing that existed was the drunk who'd shoved my dad.

'Come on then, you arsehole, come on then!' I started hitting him. 'Come on, fight!' I hit him some more. 'Sonofabitch!' The world was reduced to a man who'd shoved my dad against a column.

* * *

A few seconds ago, the only thing that existed were two policemen. Now there are also the men from years before who yelled at me, 'Fly, butterfly, fly!' The man from Steam, the one who taunted me, is back: he exists again. The men from The Letcher exist too: the one who shoved my dad against another man; and then him, the one who shoved my dad against a column. The hate swells, and as it does, time expands. 'I want to kill you. I'm going to kill you all.' And then there are the other men, the killers who wrote on a wall, 'Keep on dancing, butterflies.'

I look at the two policemen. I focus on the first one, the one who asked the question. I push him to the ground – I'm going to kill him, I'm going to kill him – but only in my head. I grab him by the neck, as I did the man in The Letcher, and I bash him ten, twenty, a thousand times against the ground. I'm going to kill him.

* * *

'You're going to kill him!' Olguita screamed. 'Oh my God, someone stop him, he's going to kill him!'

I could hear her, and yet Olguita was fading into the background.

'Fight!' I also heard. 'Fight!'

I could see a head between my hands and the head belonged to the guy who shoved my dad: having smashed it into the floor, I pulled it back towards me, yelling 'Why did you push him?' Then, in disgust and rage, I bashed his head back against the ground.

'Stop it, you hear me?! Have you lost your mind? Do something, he's going to kill him!'

The only thing that existed was that head. And the men who yelled at me years ago, 'Fly, butterfly!', and the guy from Steam who made fun of me, and the annoying drunks from the shop...

★ ★ ★

In my head, just as I'm about to kill the policeman, my dad comes back. He exists again. Hate erases time, but it also turns time back.

★ ★ ★

'Look what he's doing!' Olguita yelled. 'Oh my, oh no... I didn't know he was like this.'

In the midst of the confusion, and with the man's head still in my hands, somehow I was able to think, 'Olguita is talking to my dad.' I looked up, and there he was, terrified, staring at me.

I let go of the head, which let out a 'Sonofabitch!' as I stood up. Olguita approached the man.

'Are you alright?' she asked him.

'Never better,' the man replied. He tried to stand up but couldn't. He pointed at me and said 'Sonofabitch' one last time before crawling away.

★ ★ ★

I think about my dad. I think about how I've come out looking for food, and how I'm going to find some, and how I'll soon be with him again, both of us just fine.

★ ★ ★

'Let's go,' said Olguita, and she grabbed my arm.

Random fights had broken out here and there. From the stage, Ramón-Ramona kept repeating, 'I've called the police!' and 'That's enough!' I saw a man dragging a woman across the floor. She was screaming 'Let go of my hair, let go!' as she flailed her legs about. Two people – a man and a woman – were arguing with a young man, who was laughing at them and the whole situation. I saw a woman with her face pouring with blood, bottle in hand, threatening to slash another woman's face. Briseida was nowhere to be seen.

My dad left The Letcher without looking at me or saying a word. We'd already reached the corner when the police cars pulled up, their flashing lights bathing us in red. We carried on walking as if we had nothing to do with what was going on. We heard gunshots.

'Oh, no, no, no,' said Olguita. 'Please let them be into the air.' And then again, 'Jesus, please let them be into the air.'

My dad looked at me, then behind us, then at me again, all without saying a word.

★ ★ ★

A third policeman arrives. He asks the same thing as the others before him.

'What's that guy doing there?'

They explain, and talk among themselves.

'He went out looking for food,' I hear someone say.

'Does he have any money? Search him good.'

'I don't have any money.'

'So how were you intending to pay for your food?'

'That's what I was going out to see. Sometimes they let you buy on credit.'

'No, none of that. Give him a good searching.'

The first two walk back over to search me. They tell me to take off my shoes and socks.

'Nothing,' says the man with the mask. They take it in turns to squeeze my thighs with both hands then carry on down my legs, still squeezing.

'Nothing,' they say in unison.

They lead me over to a wall.

'I've got nothing on me,' I tell them, irritated, but they keep rummaging.

A car horn sounds.

'Ready!' comes a cry from far away, and a white light bursts forth from the same direction. 'Go on, go on.' The light is coming from a bin lorry. After a brief silence, we hear the engine start.

'Are you taking the bodies away?' I ask them.

'What does it look like?' one of them replies. 'Now get out of here.'

As I put on my shoes I overhear one of the policemen say, 'Hurry up, though.' And then, 'Let's not be such sonsofbitches…' I turn around to see what he's talking about – wondering, once again filled with hate, whether he's talking about me – and when I do, I see the lorry approaching, illuminating the decapitated heads. They're still up inside the lamplights, encased in glass. And yet now… I turn away but feel compelled to look back at them. 'What is that? What is it?' I wonder. I peer harder. It's their tongues, still spilling out of their mouths.

There's a noise.

A policeman starts vomiting. He sprays the other one,

who stumbles and trips over me. He shoots me a look, not so much of irritation as of pure rage, and says:

'Son of a...'

* * *

When, years ago, I would ask about the circumstances of my birth, my dad would sit me down beside him, or on his knee, and tell me all about the stars and the sky, and one planet in particular, which, he said, existed on the outskirts of the universe. This planet had no name, or at least not for us on earth. It was so far away that nobody had thought to name it. And this, according to him, was what made it important, because although it existed and we knew of its existence, it had no name.

It was an orphan world with no sun, plunged into perpetual darkness.

'There are lots of planets like that,' he would say, looking up at the sky and inviting me to do the same. 'Orphans of the mother star, from after the dawn of the solar system.'

To give me a sense of what life there was like, of the world that was that planet, he would recount a typical night, paying particular attention to the appearance of its inhabitants.

'Anyone there could breed with anyone else. Anyone or any*thing*, which meant there were always new creatures being born, thousands every hour, and all completely bizarre to our eyes. Every time you left your house it was like stepping into a new world.'

The landscapes in this strange order (or disorder, depending on your point of view) were constantly changing. If one night the streets were lined with trees – trees like ours, with roots, a trunk, branches, and leaves, hundreds of leaves – it was highly likely that the following night there would be new variations: a winged tree with claws at the end of its roots and black feathers, the spawn of a pine tree and a crow (and this poor tree, despite having wings, couldn't fly, for its hefty trunk prevented it from taking off). Another tree came to light – or rather to dark, since it was always night there – crowned with a giant shell, the product of the nocturnal coupling between a chestnut and a turtle (and you could see its branches poking out of the holes in its carapace, as if they were the turtle's feet). There were also occasions – and not all that infrequent – when those streets became bare. Of course, for every tree that was born and grew and stayed on, there was another that would gallop away. ('Ah,' my dad sighed, 'imagine the neigh on those horse-trees!') Or, as with the offspring of the cypress and the snake, they would slither away.

And that's how the pine and the crow were able to breed crow-trees, and the turtle and the chestnut tree had carapaced chestnuts. They could also make pine-crows and sapling-turtles respectively. And if the pine-crows grew tired mid-flight, they had to take extra care when landing, because they had shoots for feet and those shoots could take root in the ground and never let go again (the pine-crows also had to prevent other animals from munching on their leaves, which grew right alongside their black feathers). As for the sapling-turtles, my dad said some were frustrated at having been born without a shell: they felt exposed (and their canopies did little to ease their embarrassment), although it was also true that some were born with their modesty already protected by a wooden trunk. These creatures were very tall, and from a distance they looked like sideways chestnut trees lumbering around with reptile heads and feet.

It was quite common for that planet's inhabitants to plod along, whether they were turtle crossbreeds or not. They walked – all of them, so many of them – to witness the spectacle of the eternal night sky. There were the stars, very close and bright white, but also star creatures, which weren't easy to see with the naked eye. Sometimes, those down on the planet might just be able to pick out what looked like dances: a blinking, whirling light searching out another blinking, whirling light so they could come together and form something else: a bigger light, an explosion. The birth of a flame. At other times, though, they could see exactly what was going on up there, millions of light years away. Such was the vast size of some of those star creatures.

'What kinds of things might they see?' I would ask my dad, and if he was impatient to wind things up he would simply answer 'the vastness'. But more often he would reel off long descriptions of luminous creatures: a rocket-man with a tail of gas and dust who tore through the sky at the speed of light; or monster-stars, with talons and jaws.

'Whenever they heard a rumbling in the sky or sensed more light coming from above, the inhabitants would gaze up full of wonder and nostalgia.'

Whenever my dad spoke to me about the planet, he ended up inventing new inhabitants, and not all of them were born of two parents. Three, four, even ten – as many as they liked – could pair up to become the progenitors of these newly engendered creatures. He would tell me all about the burrowing reptile-cow, born of a cow, a lizard and a mole; a creature with black fur, a sturdy body, stubby legs and a ferocious snout, much longer than it was wide. It lived underground, but that didn't mean it missed out on those cosmic spectacles. In order to see them it would make a hole and peer out with its little eyes, mooing and whipping its scaly tail excitedly when it sensed the emergence of a new light overhead.

Although my dad was always coming up with weird and wonderful creatures, and usually forgetting those he'd already invented, one remained immutable in all his versions: the rocket-man, who blasted through the universe at remarkable speeds, leaving pieces of himself in the void. 'Every so often, this rocket-man would shoot past Earth. On one of his voyages, years ago, he accidentally veered off course, or maybe he decided to stay on Earth, who can say: the point is that a number of humans spotted him up there among the clouds, and as he descended along his great vaulted flightpath they shouted, "A man in the sky!" His landing on Earth filled people with a sense of the infinite possibilities up there, at the edges of the universe.'

'But we don't get crossbreeds like that here,' I said to him one night.

My dad replied with the gleeful look of someone who had waited a lifetime to hear those words.

'What do you mean we don't get crossbreeds here? Look,' and he led me to the mirror. 'Look.'

I looked and I looked and I asked, 'What? What am I meant to be looking at?'

And he repeated himself.

'Look.'

And I repeated myself.

'At what?'

And so he began pointing out the differences between us. He pointed out my eyes, comparing them to his.

'See how shiny yours are? What do they look like to you?' he said.

'I dunno, you tell me,' I replied.

My dad became fretful, and even a little annoyed.

'What do they look like? Take a good look.'

'I don't know,' I said reticently. 'I really don't know.'

Rather than spoon-feed me the answer, my dad got

down on his knees, where, still towering over me, he wrapped me in his arms and implored me:

'I need you to tell me what they look like.'

Worn down by his pleas, I finally gave him an answer.

'They're black.'

'Black like what?' he said.

And then, a memory: a butterfly.

'Black like the black butterfly,' I said, and my dad, visibly relieved, like someone who'd finally solved an equation, cried out.

'Exactly! See the mixture?'

I was riveted now.

'Yes!'

'And what else do you see? Your arms, for example. What do you see?'

'They're skinny.'

'Skinny like what?'

I didn't answer, so he jumped in.

'Skinny like the arms and antennae of the butterfly...' And so we went on. And this is how, if only momentarily, I came to be the son of a man – my dad – and the butterfly I'd remembered.

★ ★ ★

Now I don't know whether to look for food as planned or go home to my dad. How long is it since I left? I want to be with him – I begin walking home – and yet, the hunger, his hunger... I resume my search. I think about the heads, the black dots: those can't have been insects on the tongue (or were they?); they weren't stains on the glass (or were they?). I put that place out of my mind and keep walking. Is someone calling me? I keep walking.

'Wait for me!' I hear someone say. 'I was just on my way to yours.'

I turn around, wondering who it might be, then feel myself light up in relief, my whole body beaming, as I see Ramón-Ramona coming towards me.

'They're taking the bodies away!'

I run, we hug and Ramón-Ramona asks what I'm up to.

'Where do I start?' I think, and my eyes well up.

'Oh, no,' Ramón-Ramona says, wagging a finger at me. 'That's not allowed.'

I dry up inside without drying my eyes.

'I came out looking for food, but some policemen held me up,' I explain.

'And your dad?'

'At home.'

'Let's go and get him,' Ramón-Ramona says, and I'm grateful the decisions are being made for me. 'Then we'll get some food.'

Again, we pass the bodies. The lorry is still parked there, but there's also a crane, raising its metallic hand.

'Easy does it,' someone yells.

Slowly, the crane stretches out its arm, its great hand moving in towards the lorry. And over the side of that hand flops another, one made of flesh and very small.

'Drop it, drop it,' they yell again. 'Put it right there.'

★ ★ ★

On the night of the fight we walked Olguita home. Before we carried on to our house, she pulled me aside.

'You need to learn some self-control,' she told me. Then she opened her purse – sending sequins flying – took out her keys and the plastic bag, and chose a pill.

'My nerves are shot,' she said to herself. 'I think I'll take this now.'

My dad and I said goodbye and walked on in silence.

When we got home, though, I took advantage of the pitch darkness to explain myself.

'I was so livid that they pushed you.'

My dad turned towards me. Silence. I could make out the shape of him, but not the expression on his face.

Once inside, we went our separate ways, each to his own room.

'Goodnight,' I said.

'Night, son,' he replied, without looking at me this time. And it occurred to me how strange it was that my dad should go from looking at me without talking, to talking to me without looking. Lying in bed, the same bed we'd have to sell not long after, I thought not about how hungry I was, but about the man's head in The Letcher. I thought about my hands, and not about myself. And pondering the memory of that head between my hands, or rather, the memory of the man I'd smashed against the ground, I thought about how easy it is to kill. I was disappointed with myself for not being able to think any other thought.

★ ★ ★

The hand opens as if letting go of the bin bags in disgust, and they fall into the lorry. A policeman, a different one, calls over the others who searched me.

'The crane won't be any good for that' – and he points his torch into the dark. Illuminated now, the body is still swinging, still sitting on the man they turned into a swing.

★ ★ ★

We found out through Olguita that the police gunfire had indeed been shots into the air and that, unlikely as it had seemed to us, The Letcher had opened to the public the following night. There was a poster, she told us, on the door: Briseida's smiling face promising sweets for everyone, 'one for every customer, mouth to mouth'. All the same, for several nights, in a bid to avoid the people I'd fought with, my dad and I stayed at home, chatting or cooking, and also coming up with a monthly budget: optimistic accounting as always, which failed to include water or electricity. Olguita was annoyed at our decision to hole ourselves up, and tried her best to convince us to go with her to the bar.

'Look,' she said, knocking on the door one night, and she showed us a flyer with Ramón-Ramona's face on it. 'It's two-for-one.' Faced with our lack of enthusiasm, Olguita said, all fired up, 'Look, there's no way those drunkards will have any recollection of the fight now.' And when we said, 'Oh yes they will,' she turned around and began ranting and raving at us.

'Calm down, Olguita,' Pa said. 'Let's just go another night.'

'Another night, my arse!' she yelled at him, giving him the finger, and she made off towards her house.

'Wait,' Pa called. 'Wait, I think I do fancy a nice beer after all.'

Olguita turned around, her face all lit up, and she hugged her sequined purse to her body.

'Really?'

'You've twisted my arm,' he said, and then, to me, added, 'Come on, son, since there's a special offer.'

We put on our shoes and set off, Olguita sandwiched between us.

'Friends,' she said, smiling at both of us. 'My friends…'

I rested my head on her shoulder. We walked along like that.

'My friends,' she said again.

You can hear voices, whimpers. The policeman points his torch at the other side of the street. The dead body slips back into darkness – the body perched on the body – and faces appear where the light now shines: people talking, looking around.

'You're not allowed to be there,' the policeman yells. He flashes the light at the bodies again and asks his peers to switch on their torches.

'I said we need more torches,' he repeats, louder now, until they do as he says.

The space seems to widen with the new streams of light: it widens and fragments, depending on the direction of the beams. Sometimes they light up the living, and sometimes the bodies. For moments at a time, everything is illuminated. Then, when the direct light blinds me, there's nothing. In the midst of this flashing, I make out two policemen walking towards the lorry, carrying something – *something* – wrapped in black bin bags. Each of them holds one end. Then they swing the body and hurl it into the air as if playing a game of *chaza*.

'Careful, though,' someone says. 'They can still feel.'

★ ★ ★

On the way to The Letcher, Pa looked up.

'I can't get over those stars…' he said, smiling. 'What do you reckon: are they dead or alive?' he asked us, still looking at the night sky.

Olguita and I glanced at one another.

'I reckon some are alive and some are dead,' I said without much interest, and I hooked onto his arm in case he tripped over in his distraction.

Some birds flew past.

'Which star is the furthest away?'

'Who knows, Pa. That one, maybe.'

'Maybe that one over there is further away but bigger than this one here, and that's why they look the same size.'

We kept walking.

'Do you think they make a sound?' Pa asked.

'Who knows,' I said again. Olguita, I noticed, was very quiet.

'They must do,' he said in response to his own question. 'Like when the breeze catches a flame and it starts to sputter and you can hear it. I think they make that sound, only much louder.' He thought for a bit and then added, 'But why can't we hear them?'

'I guess because they're so far away... There are so many empty spaces...'

'Maybe they don't make a sound. Maybe they're made of light, not fire. When we lived over there, in the other neighbourhood, the light didn't make any noise.'

Listening to him, I remembered the rocket-man. I wanted to see him again, just as I used to, up in the sky (my eyes would be closed, but there, in my mind's eye, was the sky) leaving parts of himself in his wake. It occurred to me for the first time that the rocket-man actually had his limbs torn from him as he shot through the sky. That is, he 'shed limbs as he went. And I wanted to tell my dad that our conversation had made me think of the story he used to tell years ago when I asked him about my birth. I didn't, though, because I didn't know what to think about all the things he'd said (and not said) every time I asked. I thought, too, as we walked, that Pa was saying beautiful things, and I needed to remember them.

'There are lots of stars tonight. And the ones we don't see...'

'But there's only one,' Olguita interrupted, 'a single

star: Jesus, who rose to heaven. The others are mirrors that reflect him and each other.'

Laughter.

A drunk staggered by.

'Why so serious?' he asked as he lurched towards us. 'Let's do the conga!'

'Great idea!' Olguita said. 'You hold on to him.' And she pointed at a lamp post.

* * *

'I said you're not allowed to be there,' the policeman says, flashing his torch at the people in front of him; he moves it from side to side and their faces appear and disappear.

'Let me through. I think my friend's in there...'

'I've already told you, you can't cross this line.'

'Rudeness is your answer to everything...' another complains.

'Move along, folks!'

Then I see my dad. Is that him? I think it's him, in the crowd.

'We've got to get past,' I say to Ramón-Ramona. 'My dad's over there.'

'Move along,' the policeman keeps saying.

'Handle them with care,' someone repeats. 'They can still feel.'

And someone else echoes them.

'They can still feel.'

* * *

Once we stepped into The Letcher, Ramón-Ramona – who was at the bar, drying glasses with a cloth – beckoned me over. Before I could say hello, I received a firm telling-off.

'Any more trouble from you after the scene you made last time and you're barred.' Ramón-Ramona poured me a drink, pointed at my dad and asked, 'Is that your dad?'

I nodded.

'I noticed him leaving me a tip, that's the only reason I'm letting you in.'

The bar was dead that night. Briseida was there, but without an audience, sitting on stage with a bag of sweets. The Three Toupées – Chickpeas with his dog in tow – were at the other end of the bar. They weren't talking or even looking at each other. They just drank, vacant-eyed, straight from the bottle. Watching them, I couldn't tell if they'd just met and were shy, unsure what to say, or if they were old friends happy in each other's company and silence. Chickpeas picked up Paws.

'My baby, my little pal,' Chickpeas said, petting the dog as it drooled on Alirio, who had a white, curly ponytail protruding from the back of his balding head.

'Paws, stop that,' Chickpeas told him between strokes.

'Let him be, man. He's not doing any harm,' Simón said, and they continued drinking in silence.

My dad and Olguita sat at the bar while I gravitated towards Briseida, who was crossing and uncrossing her legs, and fanning her face with her hands, complaining about the heat. She tied up her hair, looked at the door, and then at the bar.

'I don't think anyone else is going to show,' she said, either indifferent or disappointed, it was impossible to tell. She stood up and adjusted her red plaid skirt, and I wondered, captivated, whether I wanted to be her – like her – or simply watch her. Contemplate her.

'You reckon more people will show up?' Briseida asked with a scowl.

Nobody replied.

'I'm not dancing without an audience.'

'What about us? Don't we count?' came a throaty voice. I turned around to see if the woman was talking to me, Briseida, or the whole bar. 'Pleased to meet you,' she said, 'I'm Zunilda.'

She was sitting at a table with another woman. Her lips were painted black and she was wearing a short sleeveless dress, also black. I couldn't tell her age. She might have been a little younger than my dad. Her hair was plaited but still looked unkempt.

Briseida hopped off the stage and left the sweets on the bar.

'I'm out of here,' she said, and she strode to the door.

'Come back tomorrow,' Ramón-Ramona called after her, but she left without replying.

'I see where she's coming from,' said the second woman, holding onto the table to stop it wobbling. 'Stripping's much easier with a bigger crowd.'

She took a sip of water.

'You've got such a lovely face, are you from around here?' she asked.

I smiled.

'No,' I said. Then, 'Yes.' Then, 'I just moved here.'

I scanned the room, looking for Pa. He was with the Toupées. He said something and they laughed then fell silent again. Olguita was poring over her tablets at the bar.

'Come here,' said Zunilda. 'Come, sit with us. This is Marlene.'

Marlene smiled and shook my hand.

'Sorry I look a mess. It's her fault,' she said, pointing at Zunilda. 'She dragged me out of the house with no warning.'

She was wearing a long blue skirt and a yellow shirt with oil stains on it. They both laughed.

'So now it's my fault she's such a scruff bag!' Zunilda replied, and they laughed again. 'Look at those flip-flops, what a disgrace,' and they kept laughing.

'But come and pull up a seat,' they insisted.

'I don't bite,' Marlene said, 'but she does' – and she pouted her lips in Zunilda's direction.

More laughter. I laughed too.

'Are you from around here?' I asked, just to make conversation.

'I don't even know anymore, son,' said Zunilda. 'I've been so lost…'

'Lost in the head,' Marlene confirmed, and then they laughed again.

★ ★ ★

We hop over the police cordon, but my dad isn't there.

'Are you sure you saw him?' Ramón-Ramona asks.

'Yes,' I reply, and then, 'I think so.'

I turn and look around… Nothing. I keep looking.

'No need to be so rough, for fuck's sake!'

'Let me see if my friend's over there!'

I join in.

'Thugs! Show some respect! Show some respect!' I approach one of the other men shouting and tap his shoulder.

'Excuse me, have you seen a man, more or less my height, big wide eyes, grey hair, in a white long-sleeved shirt buttoned up to the top?'

'No,' he says, and he carries on yelling.

'Thugs! Brutes!'

'We're looking for a man we saw around here a little while ago. He looks like him,' Ramón-Ramona says, pointing at me. 'What else can I tell you? He was alone. He has a sort of vacant gaze, like he's lost, or somewhere else entirely. When you speak to him, it's like he doesn't understand a thing. He has kind eyes and he walks slowly.

He was just here, we saw him a second ago.'

'No.'

More yelling. A policeman comes up to us.

'Get out of here. Stop looking for trouble,' he says.

And another, further away, joins in.

'Tell them that on the count of three, I'm drawing my gun. Tell them that.'

The crowd boos.

'One…!' cries the policeman.

I gawp at Ramón-Ramona, completely dumbstruck by what our friend has said, wanting to say, 'But my dad isn't like that,' or 'My dad understands everything.' Instead I decide to keep asking after him.

'Have you seen a man more or less my height, big wide eyes…'

Finally, after a while, a man says, 'I saw him, yeah. He was alone.'

On hearing that word again – *alone, alone* – I break down in tears and start calling out for him.

'Pa! Pa!'

And my calls merge into the others' impatient cries.

'Out! Get out of here!'

'Where are you taking them?'

'Pa!'

'Careful!'

'Show some respect!'

'Pa!'

* * *

'She's just teasing,' said Zunilda, late that same evening, 'but I really have been lost, you know? Maybe it's happened to you before that you're walking down a street looking for a number, a house, say, and you get distracted looking at someone, or something, a hole in

129

the pavement, another house, *something*, you know? Or you get distracted looking at yourself, thinking about yourself, and you walk faster, and you walk straight past the house you wanted. And you don't just pass it, you leave it blocks behind, you know what I mean? And when you realise you've missed it, the house you were looking for stops mattering for a second – just for a moment, you know – because now it's more important to get unlost, or not to get more lost, or not to go on getting lost. None of this is the same thing as finding yourself. You forget about the house you were looking for, that's what I'm talking about. You forget because you're miles from the house, out in the street – which is really the opposite of a house – and you ask yourself, "Where am I? Is it dangerous? How far off course have I gone?" Sometimes I feel like that's what my life has been: getting lost and realising I'm lost, over, and over, and over again… Losing sight of the house I was looking for.'

Marlene glanced at the oil stain on her blouse.

'I wonder how I got that?' she muttered, and scrubbed at it with a wet serviette. Zunilda turned to her.

'Girl, that stain has been there since the night I met you,' she said, before carrying on. 'Sometimes, when you get lost, the house is more in sight than ever. When you're not on the street but you feel like you're on the street and you know you're on the street: then you think about the house. But I'm talking about the moment you leave the house behind, in your head too. That's what my whole life has been about.'

'I remember playing with the local kids as a child. You know, my little girlfriends. We're heading back from the square and dropping each one of us home, all holding hands, like we're a train, you know? And each time we drop someone off, we say "Choo choo! Next!", you know, as if we're the whistle, and the driver. We say bye, wait till the girl goes into her house – or waves goodbye from the door – and then carry on along our way, making engine noises.'

'But then once – and I get all anxious just telling you – I heard the girls say, "Choo choo! Next!" but nobody got off the train. One of them said to me, "We're here, Zunilda," and I looked at the house, totally baffled, and I said "That's not my house," and everyone laughed, as if I was joking, and one of them said to me, playing her part as the driver, "Time to get off, young lady, we're running late." So I got off and went up to the house, feeling lost, you know? Utterly lost, and I turned back to my friends to see if they were laughing, messing with my head on purpose. But when I looked at them they were still in a line, none the wiser to my utter disorientation, waiting for me to wave goodbye so they could carry on along their way. So I kept walking towards the house, wondering if I was mad or if they were mad, and then I suddenly recognised the number on the door. "This *is* my house," I thought, and I waved goodbye, still feeling lost on the doorstep. Listen to me now: lost on the doorstep of my own house, completely terrified of what I was experiencing.'

* * *

'Pa!'

I see him with his back to me, in the spot where I'd been earlier. He's looking for me, too – my dad and I are searching for each other. He turns around and... can he see me? I don't know if he can see me. I wave.

'Pa!'

'Two...!' yells the policeman.

'Pa!'

Alarm spreads in his wide eyes.

'I'm not laughing at you,' said Marlene. 'I've been lost too. I've started from scratch so many times… I've made a life for myself and then unmade it again, in the shortest space of time and all over the place. I've said "yes" and then "no" to the very same things. Always like that, "yes" and then "no". People say to me, "Make up your mind, Marlene, make up your mind," but I always tell them, "I don't know, I don't know," and then I end up doing either the opposite of what I wanted, or exactly what I did want but didn't know I wanted. You wouldn't believe me if I told you, son: I left home years ago, in love with the world. I cut all contact with my family. I cut them off, for reasons I won't go into, and I made up my mind not to be anyone's mother or daughter. But, see, now I've become a mother to my friends, a daughter to my lovers… Relationships are hard work. I ran away thinking there was a big old world out there, nothing like the home where I was born, but I don't think I ever found it. I've realised, too, that we don't just arrive at a world like that: we create it ourselves. I've been lost. I went from one neighbourhood to the next. For a long time I lived up the hill, up with all the lights, but I got bored – I was working in a restaurant – so I came here. Then, one night, I nearly got killed coming out of this very bar, so I went back to the lights district, the restaurant, hating everything, including myself: I quarrelled with the owners and the other waiters, and left again in a huff. I said, "Let's wipe the slate clean," thinking sometimes you have to start afresh. But bad things always seem to happen to people like us: that's just how it is in worlds like this. I got ill, and I couldn't find a job. I was running out of savings, so I came back to this neighbourhood, right here, to The Letcher, and people I'd met maybe once before, or

not even that, said to me, "Woman, get a grip. You're lost."
I told them all to fuck off, although I was on edge, really
on edge, wondering if I was really lost or just hoping I
was. I think I wanted to get lost, I don't know… They'd
say to me, "Grow up, Marlene. Find love. You need to
grow up and love someone." I hate being told what to
do. I don't know if I want to grow up. I don't know if
I want to love someone. And I don't know if I want to
know. That's the thing, I don't know if I want to know. So
I decided to up sticks again. Yet again. I went to…'

Zunilda shut her up by putting a hand over her
mouth.

'Jesus, honey. Are you about to give us your entire
life story?'

They both laughed.

'I don't know how many times I've heard that story,'
Zunilda said to me. They carried on drinking, chatting
and teasing each other.

'You know Zunilda still gets sent flowers?' Marlene
asked me, pointing at her friend's plait. 'Probably cos they
think she's got one foot in the grave!' They laughed even
harder. But Zunilda suddenly became very serious.

'You're not lost, Marlene,' she said. 'You wander,
you've been wandering, and that's not the same thing.'

* * *

He's seen me, for sure. He's smiling. He waves.

'Stay there, Pa! I'm coming.'

At the same time, people nearby are shouting,
'Careful! Don't dump them like that!'

Pa points at his ear to tell me he can't hear.

'I said I'm coming! I'm coming!' I repeat, trying to
shout above the others. But they yell louder still.

'Don't be so rough!'

'Careful when you pick them up!'

'My friend, that's my friend!'

I look at my dad then hold out my arm, firmly, with my palm facing out, telling him not to move.

'I'm coming to you, wait there.'

I go to get him and…

'Three!' shouts the policeman, but the promised shot doesn't come.

My dad and I glance at each other. I make signs at him, but the signs he makes back only betray his confusion.

'Don't move, Pa, I'm coming.'

I'm desperate.

'I'm coming. I'm coming.'

My dad takes a few steps towards me.

'Three!' the policeman says again, and bang! A shot cracks out.

I duck. Everyone around me ducks, it seems, or throws themselves to the ground. Some lie flat on their belly with their hands over the back of their neck. I look up, searching, searching…

Then I spot my dad shuffling along, hunched, trying to reach me. I speak to him silently.

'Stay still,' I say, 'Get down. We'll find each other afterwards.'

He keeps walking. I close my eyes, keep talking to him, begging him.

'Get down, Pa, please. Get down.' But I stop when I hear the policeman's voice. 'Hey,' he yells. 'Freeze!' My dad looks at him and all I can think is, 'Pa is all alone, Pa is all alone…'

'Get out of here!' yells the policeman, and bang! Another shot. Bang! One more.

I see Pa fall. Did he fall or crouch? I gulp down a howl. My eyes explode. I remember Olguita, 'Please let them be into the air, please let them be into the air…'

People start leaving. Some say things to me under their breath, but I don't listen.

'My baby!' I start yelling. 'My baby, I don't believe it. I don't believe it!' They keep talking. A man comes up to me and says precisely the words I don't want to hear.

'They're going to say they found him dead, with the rest of them.'

I drown out that voice, which has turned my eyes into water. Ramón-Ramona comes over and grabs me by the shoulders.

'Calm down. Calm down. You need to calm down.' I want to yell, yell into Ramón-Ramona's face. I want to lash out and say 'I want to feel! Leave me be! Let me feel!' Instead I walk towards my dad, my hands resolutely clamped over my mouth. Ramón-Ramona comes with me.

Then I stop. I'm torn. I can't do it, I think, but I tell myself I'm strong. I keep going.

'Pa?' Overcome, I call out for him again. 'Pa?' And all the while I'm torn: I don't know whether to raise my voice so as to be sure the sound would reach him, or to call him quietly, very softly, so it's possible he simply hasn't heard. On the inside, I'm still shouting, 'What have you done to my baby? What have you done?' I look up at the sky and down at the street. 'Pa! Pa!'

'Right!' yells the policeman. 'Now get to work. They're leaving.'

Where's my dad? I don't want to feel. I don't want to feel. The lorry reverses and… I don't want to feel.

'Now let's get the ones over there,' says another policeman, flashing his torch at some bodies.

'Pa?' I look to one side, I can't see him. 'Pa?' I keep walking, feeling empty — empty and full of him. So full and so empty that I don't notice him coming up to us to say, 'What a fright.'

I burst with joy. I hug him. But I don't want to feel…
I caress his face.

'Baby, my baby,' I say. 'I thought you got shot.' Ramón-Ramona hugs him too, squeezes his shoulder and pats his back.

'I've scraped my leg,' my dad says.

'Don't worry,' I say. 'I'll make it better.'

★ ★ ★

'I'm having a hot flush,' Olguita said, coming towards our table. 'I think I'll head off.'

Meanwhile, Marlene and Zunilda were chatting about food, exchanging recipes, envisaging feasts.

'What I wouldn't give for a baked potato, the really tasty kind with a sprinkling of coriander,' they were saying. 'I'm craving rice and beans.' Olguita was shiny and pearled with sweat, translucent freckles all over her face. I decided to go with her, first saying goodbye to Marlene and Zunilda.

'Lovely to meet you,' I said.

'See you again, son,' they replied.

We looked for my dad, who was standing by the Toupées in silence.

'Isn't he lovely?' Chickpeas asked me, picking up Paws.

'Very,' I told him. I introduced myself briefly before leaving again, with Olguita and Pa on either side.

When we got to her house, Olguita flew off the handle.

'Real nice, eh? Coming out with me and then leaving me on my own at the bar.' We looked at her, flummoxed, unsure how to respond, so she shut down the conversation.

'Forget it,' she said. 'Don't say a word.'

At the door, without looking at us, she began groaning in pain.

'Jesus, Jesus, how long must this go on?' she asked, putting a hand on her back and arching her body. She rummaged in her bag for some pills. 'I don't know what I'm going to do,' she said in the end, and slammed the door.

Nights went by. My dad and I did some calculations and cut our daily budget — those subtractions were the very picture of our insolvency. We stayed in, unpacking the bags and boxes that contained our old home, a home in pieces following the move. My heart sank each time we removed a sheet of bubble wrap or tore up a cardboard box; each time we peeled back a piece of sticky tape to reveal a plate or a cushion out of context, like the scattered parts of a body. And yet, seeing the objects like that, in isolation, was also a reason to feel happy: each thing, each fragment, meant the possibility of creating a new place to live. Every 'This we'll keep' or 'This we'll pawn' contained, with its own joys and sorrows, the possibility of a different home.

There were also, strewn about the place, boxes full of products left over from the shop.

'If we're mindful of what we eat, we'll have food enough for a week or so,' we told ourselves.

We would stroll around our new neighbourhood and the surrounding areas — by the sea — looking for some form of amusement, for pawnshops, and sometimes even for work.

'We can come and eat here,' Pa might say, pointing at some simple café, 'when we want a change of scene, or to celebrate a special occasion.'

Those walks included an obligatory visit to Olguita, who'd been staying indoors more than usual since that night at The Letcher.

'Come on, let's go out,' we'd coax her when she opened the door.

'No, no. I don't want to, I don't feel like it,' she'd say, sending us on our way. Sometimes she'd let us come in and we'd stay and chat for a while. Other times we'd see her at the bar, on her own, after having told us she didn't feel like going out.

One night, when I got to her house – my dad had decided to stay in, arranging the cupboards and wardrobes – I saw Yadira standing under her 'Coconuts and chewing gum' sign. She told me that Olguita hadn't left the house for several nights.

'How do you know?' I asked her.

'I've been keeping an eye out,' she replied, tears rolling down her face.

I felt myself emptying out again. Did this call for tears?

'Are you alright?' I asked, and Yadira glanced at the door.

'She hasn't left the house. She hasn't left the house,' she repeated.

'Maybe she did and you didn't notice,' I suggested, mostly so I wouldn't have to think about the alternatives.

'No. I'm telling you she hasn't,' Yadira said, exasperated now. With her hand covering her forehead, face upturned, she wept, 'Oh my God, oh my God…'

'What's going on?' I was left wondering. 'What's happened? What's going on?'

I felt a thick fog trapped inside me, which slowly turned solid: a fog, or perhaps pools of unsettled water, which solidified into a kind of black jelly before melting back into fog, or water. And all the while I was telling myself, 'Maybe Olguita went out without Yadira noticing. Maybe she went out, yes. Maybe she went out.'

That thought brought me some comfort, and yet

when I heard Yadira's voice again – 'She hasn't gone out, she hasn't gone out' – the fog turned back into jelly. All the water inside me formed pools and I suddenly felt very heavy.

I rang the doorbell – nothing. Silence. Silences.

'Olguita?'

Nothing.

I started banging at the door.

'Open up, Olgui, it's me!'

And again.

'Olgui, my love, Olguita!' I turned to Yadira. 'Maybe she's worried about thieves at the door, or murderers… She must be asleep… I'm going to see if she's at The Letcher. I'll be right back.'

I was determined to find some simple reason for her not answering. I was determined not to worry just yet.

'Think you could smash the window in?' Yadira asked, ignoring what I'd just said. She passed me a coconut. 'Smash it, go on, but stand right next to the door.' I did as she said. I threw the coconut and some of the glass fell in. Then, with my shoe, I broke off the remains, feeling a rush of heat, and then another, even hotter.

'Olguita?' I called again. 'Olguita!'

'Go in,' Yadira said. 'Go on!'

I put my hand through the broken windowpane and unlocked the door.

'I don't want to do this,' I started telling myself. 'I don't want to.'

And then I said the same thing to Yadira.

'I don't want to. You go,' and I started crying.

Yadira came closer.

'You already know what you're going to find.'

'I don't,' I thought, 'I really don't.' And I said, 'You go, go on,' but then I followed her into the living room, calling out for Olguita.

'Olguita?' I cried. And then louder, out of my mind, 'Olguita, my love, are you in there?' We reached the corridor, which had three doors.

'But which one is Olguita's bedroom?'

I couldn't bear having to try each one looking for my friend. And yet I had no choice. The first one led to the bathroom.

'Olguita?'

Nothing, nobody.

'Olguita?' I called out again inside the bathroom, as if it were possible she just hadn't heard. As if it were possible I just hadn't seen her. I left the room and walked up to the second door, thinking, 'There are still two left.' Thinking, 'Maybe she's out.' And when I opened it, suddenly it hit me. Horror, more fog inside me. In the bed, a pair of feet. Olguita's feet poking out from the covers.

'No' I cried. 'No, no, no.'

I closed the door and wept.

'Oh my God. I knew it. Didn't I tell you? I knew it. Those pills, the pills!' Yadira was saying.

The fog in my body was black jelly once more, and then something else: ice, black and heavy as well. I opened the door again.

'Oh, Olguita, what's happened, my love? What's happened?'

'Close the door, son!' Yadira was screaming. And then, 'Open it!' She kept repeating the same words over and over. 'What are we going to do? What are we going to do? What are we going to do?'

★ ★ ★

'Didn't I tell you to get out of here?' the policeman yells, interrupting Pa's and my embrace.

Behind him, two men in masks pick something up: a heap of flesh, a bent leg.

The guy in uniform looks at the three of us, one by one. He remains silent, thinking, and then finally asks Ramón-Ramona, 'Don't you work in that joint?' before answering his own question, 'I remember you.'

'How much longer till we finish?' he yells at the other policemen, and he turns away from us.

★ ★ ★

We made calls to report what had happened. Before dialling, though, I wondered, anxiously, what exactly I was going to say.

'What do I tell them? How do I do it?' I implored Yadira.

Losing her patience, she pointed at Olguita.

'Can't you see?'

But I couldn't see or think anything, and I looked away, paralysed again.

'But what happened? What do I say? How should I say it?' I asked, dialling numbers in a daze. After a while I heard myself say, 'Good evening, hello, yes, I'm calling to report a death.' Then I hung up, cried, and called back. 'Good evening… I've just found my friend dead in her bed…'

And down the line came terrifying questions.

'When did you find her? How long has she been dead?'

'I don't know, I don't know,' I said, overwhelmed.

Yadira snatched the phone and replied:

'Not long, I don't think. There's no smell…' and turning to me, she said, 'Go and see what house number it is, quickly.' Being given a specific task allowed me to feel like I was helping my friend. Once I was outside, though, I forgot for a few seconds what it was I had to do. I closed my eyes and thought. 'The number.' There it was, thirty-three, up on the door, and as if to fill my mind with something other than what was going on, I walked into the house repeating in my head, 'Thirty-three, thirty-three…'

'What number is it?' Yadira asked.

And I told her, feeling calmer, 'Thirty-three.'

* * *

A man appears. He's got a shaved head and a beard.

'How long have they been here?' he asks, and I don't know if he's referring to us, the bodies or the police.

I press one finger to my mouth and open my eyes wide. And when I look at him again, I think, 'I know this guy.'

He smiles.

'Who is it? Who is it?' I think.

'Don't you recognise me?' he asks, rubbing his wrist.

'Of course I do, Lunita!' I say, relieved, having come to my senses. I kiss him, I hug her.

Further along the pavement, on the other side of the yellow tape, a policeman leans a ladder against a lamp post. He climbs up slowly, and as he approaches the glass – or rather, the head encased in the glass – he calls down angrily and impatiently to his colleagues.

'We're better off removing the whole post!'

He climbs down and starts drilling.

* * *

Yadira told me that some men would come to collect Olguita. They'd take her to a house to prepare her body, do her make-up. We were to choose the outfit they'd put her in.

'You pick,' Yadira told me. 'I can't leave the stall unattended. I'll be robbed.' Only when she left did it occur to me that I'd have to go into the bedroom to choose the clothes. But I didn't: I didn't want to have to see my friend like that. Instead, I paced around the house, thinking and crying.

'Olguita. Oh, Olguita, my love,' I heard myself say as I tried to make sense of what had happened. I also thought about my dad. I pictured the scene: me telling him, him going to pieces, both of us crying for our friend Olguita.

After a while I resolved to do whatever I had to for my friend. I entered the room and saw her – the grey-green skin, the slightly open mouth – but I looked away immediately. Something brutal was happening inside me, in my stomach.

'You will not vomit. She's your friend,' I told myself. And I obeyed. My mind turned to her eyes. I looked at her again. They were closed.

With my back to Olguita's body, I opened the wardrobe and saw her dresses. My eyes filled with tears. I chose a white one, with embroidered flowers. 'This one suited her,' I thought. I took out a headband too, with plastic cream-coloured pearls.

'My love, my darling,' I kept saying to her.

I cried some more.

Yadira called out to me and rang the doorbell.

'I've got the clothes,' I said when I reached her.

'They've come for Olguita,' she said, pointing to a van. A deeper sense of emptiness filled me. I dried up inside and began to hurry.

'All ready,' I said as an old man stepped out of the van. He opened the back doors and pulled out a stretcher.

'Where's the body?' he asked, wheeling it over.

'This way,' I said. 'I'll show you,' and I handed the clothes to Yadira.

Back in the room, in front of my friend, the old man turned to me.

'I'm going to have to ask for your help. I can't do this on my own.' He lined up the stretcher beside the bed, pulled the blanket off and took Olguita by the armpits. 'They sent me alone. There's a lot of work at the moment,' he went on. Then he gestured towards the feet, the red toenails. 'You take that end,' he said.

'I can't,' I thought. Then, 'I'm not allowed to feel disgusted.' Then, 'This is what Olguita needs from me right now.' I took her by the ankles. She was stone cold.

'On the count of three,' the old man said. 'One, two…'

I picked her up, but the old man had misjudged her weight, and practically dropped her. There was a thud, and both Olguita's arms were left dangling.

'Be careful, come on,' I say, crossly.

Without looking at me or apologising, the old man covered her with the sheet.

On the way back to the van – with him and Olguita – I felt an itch on my face. I didn't scratch it. I felt – to my shame – that before scratching my face I needed to wash my hands.

* * *

They put more body parts into bin bags. To do so, they wear yellow gloves. Every so often they grumble and bark orders at each other.

'That's not my job,' one of them says.

'Oh, is that right? Whose job is it then?' replies another, adjusting his mask.

I want to leave, to see something else.

'Let's go, why are we still here?' I say.

My dad looks at me and, ignoring my request, or

perhaps not having heard it, he replies, 'I wonder what happened to the cockerel? It was alive that night.'

★ ★ ★

When the old man started the engine, I wasn't sure whether to run and give my dad the news, or to stay with Olguita – to keep her company. I was terrified they might lose her or do something to her: do her make-up all wrong, kill her again. In the end I decided to go to my dad.

'Sir,' I called out to the old man. 'She wore her hair down and brushed back with a headband. And she didn't wear much makeup, just pale pink lipstick. Please, look after her.'

'Don't worry. We will.'

'Thank you.'

'She'll look lovely.'

He reached out a hand to give me his card and I was scandalised at the exchange: the informality, the flippancy.

'I'll stay here,' Yadira said, and she started to cry. Overcome with emotion, feeling awkward, I patted her on the back a few times.

'That's enough now,' I said. 'That's enough.' And then, contradicting myself, 'Cry all you want, Yadira.' I left her, promising I'd come back with my dad.

On my way home, worried about how he'd react, I imagined myself saying, 'Pa, something has happened and you need to be strong. Olguita died.' And because I wasn't satisfied, or convinced, I kept practising.

'Pa, we can't fall apart… Pa, I'm sorry to tell you that Olguita died. We found her dead in her bed, Yadira and I. We don't know what happened.'

In different versions of the conversation, I saw myself saying, 'Our friend, our friend!' before bursting into tears.

When I got there, I opened the door carefully to maintain the silence. I didn't want him to hear me enter. I wanted, yes, to delay breaking the news.

'Is that you?' I heard him say. 'You're late.'

And as soon as I saw my dad – his suffering gone – the pain came flooding out of me.

'What's the matter?' he asked, coming over. 'What did they do to you?'

I started telling him, but he couldn't make sense of what I was saying.

'Did someone take a dig at you at the bar? Did you get into a fight? Who took a dig at you?'

And I shook my head. Then I said it again. I repeated myself, but my dad still didn't understand.

'Calm down and tell me,' he said, walking to the kitchen. 'Have a glass of water.' Resenting him for not understanding what I was trying to tell him – irritated, in despair at having to repeat what I never wanted to say – I ended up yelling.

'I said Olguita's dead!'

I watched my dad become a statue of himself.

In perfect silence, he exploded, growing greyer.

'But how?' he asked. 'How do you know? How did she die?'

I told him, and as we spoke, I felt my face morph in response to my dad's pained expressions. We were both beside ourselves, disfigured by grief.

'Where are we going to bury her?' Pa asked. 'How?' I showed him the card the old man gave me and he began fussing, saying we needed to call him. We headed to Olguita's place and, on the way, as if only just remembering how poor we were, I regretted not having a phone.

When we got to the house I was surprised that Yadira wasn't there. Her stall wasn't on the corner, either. I was even more surprised, on walking through the front door, to find the 'Coconuts and chewing gum' sign lying in the middle of the living room.

'Who's there?' she shouted.

'It's us.'

She came out of the hallway holding a bundle of dresses.

'I just thought I'd take these,' she explained. 'Gifts from my old friend.'

I glared at her in disgust and rage, then stormed off to look for the phone.

'Otherwise who knows where they'll end up,' Yadira went on.

★ ★ ★

I remember how hungry I am.

Or rather, my hunger reminds me it's still here. A whirlpool is what I feel, a whirlpool of pain and emptiness that pulls me out of the world without pulling me out of my body. A force that reduces the whole world to my body. An ache that makes me gigantic.

'I need to eat something.'

Ramón-Ramona looks at me. Luna too. Then they look at a policeman flinging bags onto the lorry. I look at my dad to avoid their stares – what they say, what they're getting at – and ask him, desperate now, 'Aren't you hungry?'

'Don't worry, son,' he replies.

★ ★ ★

We made calls, we discussed prices. When one of us felt like the conversation was becoming too much we passed the phone to the other: my dad to me, me to him.

'There's a lot of work at the moment,' the funeral

directors informed us. 'Not enough coffins.' My dad wanted a specific kind of casket – wooden, elegant and pretty. I didn't care either way.

'I'm looking at a purple one, brand new,' one of them told me.

'They say they have a purple one,' I repeated to my dad.

'Oof, no, no, no,' he said. 'I don't like that colour for Olguita.'

He snatched the phone.

'Can't I make my friend's coffin myself?'

I turned to him agape, but he carried on before I had time to think of what to say. 'We can use the slats from the bed and some cardboard. We'll do a lovely job of decorating it.' I couldn't decide whether it was a good idea or totally insane. 'We'd bring our own coffin,' he insisted, trying to persuade the person. 'We'll start making it right now. My son's here, he'll help me.'

Outraged, Yadira started shouting.

'There's no time for that. Stop all this scheming.'

My dad's face went blank. He looked at her, then at the ground. Yadira went on:

'We don't know how long she's been dead, the poor thing! We need to bury her now.'

My dad passed me the phone.

'We're very busy,' the undertaker said, uninterested, on the other end of the line. 'There's a lot of work.'

'So give us the purple casket,' I said, while Yadira continued:

'We need to bury her now. Poor thing, poor thing!'

'Excellent choice,' they replied. 'We'll send some flowers along with her, at no extra cost.'

* * *

'It's already full,' the driver yells. 'How much more to go?'

'All that, look,' the policeman replies, and he nods his head at a dead, pitch-black street.

There's a noise. Like cogs turning, like a factory. Or shutters opening.

'That's it!' yells another. 'Pack 'em down, pack 'em down.'

The driver smiles and gives a thumbs-up through the lorry window.

★ ★ ★

Before setting off to the place where they'd put Olguita – a narrow, dirty parlour in some forgotten corner of the neighbourhood – we made hazy decisions, one by one: we'll go home, maybe, have a shower, maybe, change our clothes.

'We'd better smarten up,' Pa may have said. 'We're going to say goodbye to a friend.' I dressed in black; he, in white and blue.

As soon as we got to the funeral home, I spotted the coffin, which was indeed purple and had two plastic roses on top, each in a little vase. A woman was bent over the body, crying. From time to time she wailed, 'Oh, my friend! My friend!' and tapped her head against the coffin. My dad looked around as we walked to the middle of the room. The walls were tiled in green from floor to ceiling, like a bathroom.

The woman hunched over the glass in such a way that she covered Olguita. I put my hand on her shoulder.

'Excuse us, please,' I said.

She stopped crying immediately, clearly flustered.

'Go on, yes. Look at her,' she said, as if woken from a trance.

My dad went first. He looked. Then he looked harder.

He stepped away from the casket and then took a step closer again.

'I can't see anything.'

'What do you mean?' I asked, drawing in closer.

The glass was steamed up.

I ran my finger over it. Nothing.

'It needs to be wiped from the inside,' the woman said. 'If you want we can open it and wipe it.'

'Let's do that,' I heard myself say.

Between the two of us we lifted the lid and... Olguita.

'Olguita, my love!'

I broke down.

'Those pills,' the woman said. 'The pills!'

My dad stepped back from the coffin.

'Olguita!' cried the woman, or perhaps it was me. 'Look at you!'

Her face was all blotchy, covered in colours that the make-up couldn't conceal: shades of purple and yellow. They had stuck her lips together with glue, or so it seemed. Her mouth looked taut, pulled into a forced smile. And they'd done her hair with a bow, and not with the headband the way I'd asked them to. And the dress, like her face, was all stained.

It was a conscious decision to lose it; it was my way of trying to trick the pain. I wanted that other emotion to overshadow my suffering.

'I told them she wore her hair down,' I said to the woman, raising my voice. 'I explicitly told them that.'

She had calmed down a little.

'Do you have anything to wipe the glass with?'

I checked my pockets: nothing.

'No matter,' she replied. 'I'll use my hand.' And so, with her bare hand, she started to wipe the condensation off the glass.

★ ★ ★

'Chuck it in there! It'll fit in there!' comes a voice. Then, soaring gracefully through the air, a black bin bag.

It crashes with a thud into the mouth of the lorry, which opens and closes hungrily.

'Let's go, come on,' I plead again. 'What are we doing here?'

No one moves.

★ ★ ★

'And just look how grubby they've left her,' I went on complaining. 'The dress, all covered in stains.'

'No, son,' the woman said. 'That's the water that comes out of them.'

My dad came over to us. He was with three other women now.

'I let this lot know,' Yadira spouted proudly as she entered the room. 'And there are more people on the way.' Then she peered through the glass, grimaced and cried. The others sat down on plastic chairs.

'There aren't many people here at all,' said Pa.

'Go on, say goodbye to her. We've wiped the glass.'

'I'll be right back,' Pa said.

As soon as he left I sat down to wait for him. Exhausted, I stared at the coffin, but, still plagued by anxiety, I kept wondering if I should go and stand next to it or stay seated. Sitting there I felt a long way from Olguita. but even right beside the coffin I didn't feel like I was by her side. I stayed seated.

The women, meanwhile, chatted away loudly.

'Lord Jesus, please give her a big hug up there! Take her in your arms, raise her up!'

Another woman seconded her.

They cried, they laughed. They also wondered about the house.

'What'll happen with it?' I heard them ask, before turning the conversation back to God and how lonely Olguita had been.

After what seemed like a long time, my dad came back, carrying a box. Yadira went up to him.

'What have you brought?' she asked. She looked inside and then answered her own question, 'A box full of crap.' Pa glared at her.

'Come and give me a hand,' he said to me, and I followed him, ignoring Yadira. He handed me the box.

Then he gave the coffin a little tap, as if he were paying Olguita a visit.

'The best friend you could ask for,' he said loudly, before pulling out a rusty copper medal bearing the image of an eagle. On a small piece of card he'd written 'Olguita, the best friend you could ask for' and it was pasted onto the insignia.

My dad took the medal, kissed it and placed it on top of the glass.

'Thank you, sister,' he said. He also took out some fake flowers, which he scattered around the coffin. Lastly, he took out some paper and crayons. 'Let's draw Jesus,' he said to me, and together we drew a picture of Jesus and Olguita, the two of them walking along the water's edge. We placed the portrait between the plastic roses.

★ ★ ★

They fling another bag into the lorry. And another.

'Easy!' a policeman cries. 'You nearly dumped that on my head!'

I pull tired faces and look at the others.

'I don't want him to watch this,' I say, pointing at my

dad. 'You know how he gets, that thing that happens to him.'

'It already did. Can't you see? He's out the other side now,' Ramón-Ramona says.

'You don't know that.'

'Leave your dad out of it. The one who doesn't want to be here is you.'

I lose it. Why on earth would I want to be there?

★ ★ ★

I felt night fall in my own being.

'Those pills!' the women went on. 'Those pills!'

I looked for a seat and I cried again, covering my face. I don't know if I was crying because Olguita had gone, or for the fact of having met her at all. I felt ashamed, and the shame overrode all other emotions.

My dad sat beside me. He seemed calm, albeit spaced out, unsure what to do with himself. He rested a hand on my thigh. I was worried he might have a relapse. I told myself I needed to stay calm and avoid anything that might drag him down again, sending him back to his bed for nights on end. I thought about Olguita. I cried. And I thought about myself.

More women filed in. One of them was holding a young boy by the hand. Together they went up to the coffin and the sight of it made them cry out.

'What's in there?' the child asked.

I turned away. Then, suddenly, as if he'd just had an idea, or thought of something that might console me, my dad whispered in my ear.

'See her?' he asked, pointing at the woman with the child. 'That's what your mum looked like.'

I stared at him blankly as if I'd just been blinded. Then the boy did something – asked a question, or played a game – which made the woman smack him on the head. I snapped out of my daze.

'Oh, dear. But not like that. More like her,' and he pointed at another woman who was crying. 'No, she looked more like her,' he added, looking at yet another. I closed my eyes.

★ ★ ★

Another black bin bag, flying through the air, forming an arc.

How many more are there?

How many more?

It lands in the lorry.

Another, immediately afterwards, smashes against the tyre.

'Look lively, boys!' the driver yells. 'The whole lot fell out.'

How many more?

★ ★ ★

Several thoughts later, I opened my eyes. My dad was standing beside the coffin, talking to Olguita. Beside me was the woman who'd wiped down the glass: the first to arrive, and the one who'd wailed the loudest. As soon as she saw me shift in my seat, she began talking.

'I've lost three loved ones in the space of a year.'

I stared at her, unsure what to say.

She dragged her chair to face me and went on.

'I'm crying for all of them. My mum was taken first, in a flash. Some disease, something in her blood. I was with her. I stayed with her. We got to say goodbye. Then, about three weeks later, my daughter died. They killed her. She killed herself. I don't know. She was found dead, anyway, with a fractured arm. They told me it was her but I don't know. I didn't recognise her – I couldn't, or I didn't want to – when I went to identify her. They kept saying to me, "It's her, lady. It's her," in that horrible room. They asked, "Were your daughter's teeth straight or crooked?" "Straight," I said, over and over again, but the body they were showing me had crooked teeth. They kept telling me, "It's her, lady, believe us." And who knows. Maybe it was. Sometimes I think maybe Nuria did have crooked teeth after all, and that when I saw the body with teeth like that I got it into my head that her teeth were straight. As I say, I don't know. If only I had a picture… Oh, God! And now it's my friend. Olguita helped me out so much, son. She gave me money, food. We met on the street, I think, or at the bar, not long after I wound up alone. She noticed me crying and asked me what was wrong. I told her about my daughter. She told me about Jesus. I also told her about my mother. She said, "It's terrible what you've had to go through, pet." Then told me about her own losses. First she said, "You forget." And then, "You never forget, but you embrace it." And I said, "Oh, love. Sometimes I go to bed thinking they're alive. I forget, for a few seconds! And when I remember…"'

The door opened. Through it came a man in an undershirt and the old man who'd collected Olguita. They asked for my dad and went over to speak to him. His face grew even sadder. I asked him what was wrong.

'We have to bury her now,' was all he said, stroking the purple coffin.

★ ★ ★

'Last one, last one!'

They throw the last bag into the lorry and then gleefully remove the yellow police tape.

'Done and dusted,' someone says.

They cheer, and leave. None of them looks at us.

I ask my dad if the scrape on his knee hurts. He says it's OK. I ask him if he's hungry. He says he isn't. I despair again. Luna asks us to come with her. She wants to hang around a bit longer – even longer! – and take a stroll through the bar district.

'Of course, darling,' Ramón-Ramona says, begging me, with a look, for patience.

We set off slowly, and as they talk and grow depressed and bemoan all those deaths – 'So many,' they say, 'and so young!' – I put my arm around my dad. I rest my head on his shoulder, and we walk. I can hear his every breath, feel his every move. He's sweating and his skin is hot. He's moving. My dad is moving. I think about the gunshot: in my mind's eye I see him fall. I think about Olguita: her cold skin when I had to carry her. My dad is sweating and his skin is hot. I squeeze him tighter.

'Their whole life ahead of them,' Luna goes on, 'and just like that, someone kills them.'

I feel irritated.

'So if they'd been about to die just before they were killed, if they'd only had one night left anyway, then it wouldn't be so bad?' I ask her, looking away.

'It's always sad, but someone who dies older has already lived their life.'

I think about Olguita, who died older. I think of my dad, who's older. I think about myself. What can you do in a single night? Everything. So much. One night is a lifetime. I turn to Luna:

'Just because they're older it doesn't necessarily mean they've lived their life.' My dad squeezes my arm: to let me know I'm right, maybe, or to ask me to be quiet.

'This one likes a fight,' says Ramón-Ramona, pointing at me.

156

'So I've been told,' I say.

Then we fall silent.

It's windy.

We keep walking until we reach the wall. 'Keep on dancing, butterflies.'

'So cruel,' Luna says.

She begins to cry.

I look at her, imagining her without a beard: I see Luna in the limelight, singing up on the stage, blowing kisses to the people who are gone. And I picture the crowd yelling, 'Luna! Luna! One more tune, one more tune!' – an ovation from those no longer with us. And the heckles, too. I don't forget the heckling.

Then, the wall before us... I look at it. I defy it. It's still bleeding.

'Keep on dancing,' I read. Then, 'Butterflies'.

★ ★ ★

We carried Olguita's coffin between us – the old man, my dad, Yadira and I – each of us holding one corner. It was heavy. Heavy in every sense. We set it down on a sort of wheeled stretcher so we could push it.

'Where's the grave?' the woman with the child asked.

'Over there,' said the old man. 'Over there.'

We kept pushing.

At the grave, the man in the undershirt was waiting for us.

'Put it down here,' he said hurriedly, pointing at some ropes.

We did as he asked and the old man moved a lever: the coffin – Olguita – began to descend.

'Hold me back!' Yadira screamed, upsetting us all. 'Hold me back or I'll jump into that pit with her.' The woman lunged to stop her.

'Calm down, petal,' she said. 'You'll make yourself ill. Calm down.'

But Yadira kept on wailing.

'Hold me back, hold me tight! I'll throw myself in, I'm throwing myself in.'

The whole thing seemed grotesque.

I looked away and in the distance I saw a woman running towards us. She was waving, as if to say hello. For a moment I thought she might know Olguita: perhaps she found out late, and was only now getting to the burial. The man in the undershirt called out to the old man. He said, 'Florinda's coming,' and as soon as he saw her, the old man stopped moving the lever.

We waited.

'Have you paid for this?' she asked, out of breath, when she finally reached us.

'No,' I thought, but I said, 'Yes, of course.'

My dad's eyes opened wide. I noticed the child was playing with the soil.

'Show me the receipt,' the lady asked me, so I started checking my pockets, acting natural.

'I don't have it on me. I'm sorry.'

Florinda made a sign, and they started to pull the coffin back up.

'Hang on,' Yadira came up to us. 'You mean we're not going to bury her?'

'You have to pay.'

'But we've already paid,' I kept saying.

The woman turned away from me, deciding to speak only to my dad.

'I've got interested customers queuing up,' she said. 'A long line of people wanting a grave. I'm very sorry, sir, but if you don't pay you can't bury her here.'

'Whatever you do, don't cremate her,' Yadira begged. 'That's like killing her twice.'

They discussed prices. My dad did the talking, the negotiating, throwing glances at Olguita resting on the ropes as he did sums with his fingers.

'Pa,' I tried again. 'I paid already, remember…'

He held up his hand to stop me. They went on talking. Meanwhile, I was distracted by the sight of Olguita suspended there, unable to feel a thing.

I don't know how long it was before Florinda spoke.

'Perfect, that's a deal then,' she said, snapping her fingers at the old man.

And Olguita descended once more.

★ ★ ★

'Keep on dancing…'

I think about all the men who've called me that – 'Butterfly, butterfly!' I think about them, and about my dad, too, as if he's far away, as if I didn't have my arm around him now. I go back to the night when he made me the son of the butterfly I remembered.

They can inflate in the wind, butterflies: they absorb it, swallow it, and then they grow, their wings swell, becoming up to fifteen times bigger. At night they hang from the leaves, upside down, hiding in the foliage. No one knows if they sleep or not, but they rest. Butterflies can make love while flying. They tend not to, but they can. So if something, or someone, bothers them in the act, they take flight. Sex lingers in the air.

I also remember my eyes. 'They're black,' I told him. And he said, 'Black like what?' From my mouth came the answer he wanted, 'Black like the black butterfly.'

Standing before the wall, I thank my dad – in silence, and unbeknownst to him – for forcing me to remember, to create, my own origins.

'It seems unreal,' Luna says, now facing away from the

wall. 'As if nothing had happened.'

Leaves flurry in the air.

'Do you want to eat something?' I asked Pa, contorted by hunger myself.

'Don't worry, son. We'll eat soon.' My body squirms, I've had enough – and inside, a scream.

'Keep on dancing, butterflies.'

I look up at the sky, at the streets. Sex lingers in the air.

CHAPTER V

Versions of the Night

We set off home from the funeral. I was brimming with black ice and didn't want to think. The boy kicked me.

'Catch me if you can!' he said, and started skipping around the graves.

I ignored him and kept walking. He came back.

'Don't you want to play with me?'

His mother grabbed him, gave him a pinch and tugged on his hair.

'Stop being a pest,' she said. 'I've had enough of you. Just stand still for a second.'

The boy put on a sad face but straightaway started playing with a stone.

I cast my eye around for my dad: he was walking with his head down. He glanced up and looked around for me too, perhaps sensing my unease.

'Let's go home,' he said.

We walked through the bar district. Every time the light touched us – all different neon lights, shaped like naked men, a match being struck – I glanced at my dad out of the corner of my eye, trying to interpret how he might be feeling, scared that all of this might send him back to bed. Yet when we got home – to the home we'd built from the remains of our old apartment – I was the one who holed myself up in my room, after Pa said, 'All this will have to go,' pointing at the paintings and furniture. 'We need to pay off the funeral.'

And from my bed – where I lay paralysed for nights on end, out of myself, almost someone else entirely in my state of indifference, unwilling to find out if I wasn't moving because I couldn't or because I didn't want to – I could hear my dad muttering to himself: 'This is going. And this. All this has to go.'

He kept storming into my room, and then, not quite knowing what to do, he'd hover and say something like, 'We're poor, but let's not be too glum,' and come and stroke my face. He'd smile, an empty smile, thinking he was cheering me up as I looked at him and felt empty. Sometimes he tried to stand me up – he picked me up, that is – or he sat in silence, keeping me company at the foot of the bed. He brought me tins of tuna and soup.

'Thanks, leave it there,' I'd say, without looking at him, and he'd leave the room crestfallen and confused. I'd go back to sleep, or close my eyes, and in my dreams I thought I could hear the sound of furniture creeping around.

My back started hurting one night, or maybe it had been hurting for some time but it wasn't until then that I decided to get up, or was able to. I remembered the sofa in the living room, the firm cushions, and I got out of bed to go and lie there for a change. But when I opened the door, I saw nothing but the two chairs, a table and a fan. I started looking for my dad with the feeling that our house wasn't a home any more. It was just a space.

I went to the kitchen: he was nowhere to be seen. Next, to his room: in the middle of the mattress there was nothing but a tangle of covers. Alarm bells rang inside me. The memory of Olguita. I opened my eyes – my whole body – and started calling out for him. 'Pa?' I went to the bathroom. 'Pa?' Silence. I opened the door, stepped out onto the street: there was barely a breeze. And a light, far away; the other houses. 'Are you there?' I started yelling. 'Pa?' Then I stopped. Clarity at last. His room, the bed. I walked back to his door and there he was: a great lump in the middle of the mattress, bundled up in the sheets.

'Pa, what's wrong?'

'I don't know why she got so angry,' came his voice.

I lay down by his side, trying to make sense of what he was saying.

'Who, Pa?'

'Olguita.'

Her image flashed before me again, in the coffin – the forced smile, the atrocious makeup. I closed my eyes.

Nights went by, time passed.

My dad and I kept ourselves to ourselves for a while.

'Remember to eat well, drink lots of water,' I'd say to him.

'You too. You too,' he'd reply, tangled up in the covers.

The power had been cut but, following Olguita's advice, we'd reconnected the cables.

'If it were up to us, we wouldn't do it,' the men from the electricity company had said when they came knocking. 'But there's nothing to discuss: orders from above.' The one speaking held up some pliers, and his colleague the unpaid bills.

'I understand,' my dad had said. 'I understand, don't worry,' and as soon as they left, we connected the cables again with rubber glue.

Because we could no longer turn on the lights in the rooms facing the street – so the electricity people didn't see we'd tampered with the connection – the house felt smaller. The darkened living room made it look like the street began as soon as we stepped out of our bedrooms.

'This light,' my dad would say, looking at any of the lit bulbs, 'is in loving memory of our friend.'

One night, the two of us were sitting in the living room – thinking, perhaps, about how to eke out a living, and where or how to find work – and my dad piped up:

'Give me a hug every now and then, won't you? Let's be of one heart sometimes.' He stood up from his chair and compared the brightness in the bedrooms on the other side of the apartment with the darkness where we were.

'It's so black,' he said. 'This place is like a cave.' He switched on the light – it engulfed me – and we found ourselves surrounded by white walls.

'Switch it off,' I said. 'Switch it off, we're going to get caught.'

'Don't worry, it'll be alright,' my dad replied, and went to his room looking for something to draw with. He came back shortly afterwards with clenched hands. 'There wasn't much,' he said. 'Just this black crayon.' He put it in his mouth like a cigarette.

Then he went into the kitchen and on the wall he drew two black circles, one on top of the other, and two triangles for the ears. He added a tail, coiled like a spring, and for a face two dots – the eyes – and a smiling curve.

'All that's missing is the nose,' Pa said, and he drew a nose: two dots, like the eyes, only bigger. Once he'd finished, he pointed at the sketch and said, pensively, 'Cow'.

Then he went to my room where, as if gauging what he needed for his next creation, he stood contemplating the ceiling. He tried to touch it, clambering onto the bed, but he still couldn't reach. He asked me to bring him a chair. His idea was to put the chair on the bed and then climb on top of it. I, however, asked him to forget the whole idea.

'You could fall, Pa. You could split your head open,

break your hip. Come on, the chair might break. We don't have furniture to go around breaking.'

Clearly annoyed at my response, he turned his back on me and began drawing on the wall next to the door: a circle, again, and some lines for a torso, arms and legs. Above the stickman, he wrote: 'Pa'.

'Love you, son,' he said.

With our arms around each other we went to his room, and there he drew another tiny body in the exact spot where the light shone – the light that was never turned out, since Pa was scared of being plunged into total darkness. And with the black crayon he drew a heart around the little man.

'You, my darling,' he said, and kissed me on the forehead. I sensed it was time to say something, show him some affection, even support his creative venture, so I stared at the portrait in silence, mimicking the way he'd stared at the ceiling.

'You know,' I said finally, 'it makes me want to tear out this piece of wall, frame it, and hang it right back up again, like a painting.'

My dad listened to me, perplexed but gratified, and carried on drawing: a square now, and a triangle on top.

'Do you see?' he asked. 'The roof.'

He drew the windows and doors of the house – three rectangles in different sizes – and above it all, in the sky, he magicked up a half moon.

'I don't like it,' Pa declared. 'It looks like a banana.' So he added clouds, and stars.

'Much better,' he said at last, still pensive, like a haughty perfectionist.

'The house looks nice,' I said. 'All it's missing now is us.'

'No, no. Look.'

He drew some curves and lines: three rocking chairs. Next, a circle above each chair, and although he gave them all smiley faces, only one he decorated with curls.

'You, me and Olguita, talking about life,' he said.

Then, in the living room, and in the hallway near the door, my dad drew buildings, scores of them, sprouting out of each other and forming clusters all around and above us.

'The city,' he said, 'the electric forest. Because it's still there. Even if it feels like we're far away.'

Nights went by. Time passed.

'Let's go out, but we're not to spend any money,' I'd say to my dad, or he'd say to me.

Sometimes we remembered Olguita. 'She's missing this lovely fresh breeze,' we'd say. Or, forcing ourselves to be sad: 'Boy, if only she were here.'

The way to The Letcher was dark, as dark as Lights Avenue, but as we drew near, other bar signs came into view, many of them flashing, as if there were paparazzi at the end of the street: Burn, Labyrinth, The Lanky Whale...

The only sign with no lights was the one on The Letcher. 'The cheapest bar,' my dad would say.

A new bouncer had started working there. 'Good evening,' he said, all smiles on his first night on the job. 'Come on in, it's safe here,' and he showed us his gun. I noticed the signs on the door: 'No machetes.' 'No firearms.' 'Love thy drinking partner...' We went in, my dad and I. It smelled of cleaning products.

'Long time no see!' someone called out. It was Yadira. She staggered over and started chatting to us, one arm wrapped around a column. 'Where have you been, strangers?' She hiccupped and scratched her forehead. 'Hey, strangers! Did you hear what happened with the house?' She tried to stand up straight, letting go of the column. We had to grab her and prop up her on a chair, but as soon as we did, she slumped down again, determined to lie on the floor. 'Some of Olguita's relatives turned up and took everything. Bastards!'

I left her and my dad to it, and went to the toilet. I got sidetracked reading the graffiti on the walls: 'Ramón-Ramona has a dick', 'Ramón-Ramona has a fanny', 'Kill yourself', 'Die', 'Go to hell'. There were also doodles: erect penises, mainly, but also flowers and guns. And more messages: 'This toilet won't flush', 'Briseida is a bitch', and 'Free BJs' with a phone number underneath. 'Down with the rich!' 'When you've done your business, please flush'. In a corner and in all caps: 'GOD IS HERE'.

When I came back, Yadira was asleep on the floor. Every so often she'd kick out, or open her eyes and mumble expletives before dropping off again. Meanwhile, Ramón-Ramona at the bar was complaining about the competitors, especially the bargain prices at Labyrinth, and wondering whether or not to change The Letcher's name. On top of it all, there was that new club opening soon.

'It'll be directly opposite, over by those two houses.' And to demonstrate how desperate the situation was, Ramón-Ramona showed us the (very few) bank notes in the till.

'Don't worry, pet,' Pa said. 'We're loyal customers.' He pointed to himself and me.

'Yeah, but you never buy any drinks!' Ramón-Ramona said.

Nights went by. Time passed.

The club finally opened under the name of Luna, and I went there one night when there was no entry fee.

'Go and have some fun,' Pa said. 'You won't get these years back.'

And that's what I did: I put on my best T-shirt – white with black roses on each shoulder, sewn on by me – and walked down a gloomy Lights Avenue until I reached the club's golden saloon doors.

There was a white moon — with eyes, smiling — painted on the doors where they met in the middle, and every time someone went in or out, the moon split in half. I watched it for a while, killing time, or maybe genuinely waiting for the moon to wax full, but someone always came and pushed the door open again, breaking it in two. The whole night it was halved, that white and broken moon. I walked through it.

I felt all eyes on me, lustful or curious. I heard conversations: men who yelled without yelling, who came from another part of town, up in the lights.

'I bet that one is from around here,' they'd say, as they pointed at someone sniggering. And I'd memorise their faces, to be sure to give them the cold shoulder if they hit on me later.

'What *is* this place?' they'd ask. 'What is it? Come on, let's go.'

'No, no. Let's stay.'

I danced my way through the crowd. '*Hands in the air!*' went the song. '*Hands to the floor!*' And: '*Shimmy dem hips, cos here comes the apocalypse!*' The men carved out paths with their conga line, only to abandon them. Up above, Luna ruffled her skirt and from time to time mimicked sucking off her microphone.

'Mmm, yum!' she crowed, her voice booming across the place, her big heart spilling over. 'So smooth!'

And then there was silence: no more light or music. Everything was black. Someone booed but was shushed by the crowd, as if everyone else already knew what was about to happen. Then Luna, who was still invisible, spoke up.

'No one goes home tonight without touching some cock.'

Clapping, heckling.

The lights came on again, followed by the song:

'*Shimmy dem hips, cos here comes the apocalypse!*' And at the front, on the stage, appeared nine men or maybe more, dressed in bathrobes.

'Right, so this is what's going to happen,' Luna went on from above, looming over the floorboards. 'These boys here are going to dance for us and get their kit off. And you lot – every single one of you – are allowed to touch them.' The crowd was going wild. 'And listen,' Luna said. 'They've been warned: if they can't get it up, they don't get paid.' The spotlights were on the dancers; the rest was darkness. For ages the only thing that existed was them – glistening, sweating, their hands behind their heads, and their hips shaking – grinding the air, or the darkness. Grinding the night – making love to the night – and the night was the rest of us.

'Get your kit off!' yelled Luna, and the crowd started whooping. The men removed their bathrobes with their backs to the dancefloor – a little dance, then 'Down, down to the ground,' and they turned to face us with their hands cupping their cocks.

'Hands in the air!' Luna cried. 'This is a hold up!'

'Oooh!' went the crowd when the men raised their arms, pretending to be shocked, encouraging the rest of us.

'Shimmy dem hips!' There was laughter, lust.

'Like I said,' Luna went on, 'No stiffy, no pay!' The men started to toss themselves off: one guy's cock – and this amazed me – was so long, still flaccid, that he could wave it about like a length of rope.

'He's gonna lasso us!' someone yelled and several others laughed.

'Tie me up, cowboy!'

On the dance floor, a man said something to me I couldn't hear.

'What did you say?' I replied without interest, my eyes on the show.

'Are you having a good time?'

I looked at him, then at the dancers – they were hard now, standing at the edge of the stage.

'Go on, go on! Get in there,' Luna cried to the men, and then, turning to the audience, added, 'Enjoy!'

Whooping, clapping.

The men hopped off the stage and weaved their way through the crowd.

'I said are you having a good time?' the man asked me, louder. I looked at him again, irritated now, and eyed him up: moustache, grey hair, long-sleeved shirt. I thought, 'He's not from around here.' I said, 'Great, and you?' He told me he was hungry and had to go. Meanwhile the performers were approaching. They kissed and were kissed; people grabbed their cocks… I had an idea.

'Yeah, I'll come with you,' I said. 'I'm hungry too.'

We left, slicing the moon again. He told me his name was Caiman.

'I don't know this neck of the woods,' he said, and he looked at me, smiling.

'There are a few shops nearby.'

We walked. He tried to hold my hand.

'No,' I said.

'Is it dangerous around here?'

I thought 'Yes', but said 'No', still without looking at him, and we carried on looking for a shop. All the while I was thinking how to pull off my idea without having to fuck him – I didn't want to fuck him.

'It's really dark around here,' I heard him say.

We walked past Nocturne and saw a street stall.

'They sell pies there,' I told Caiman.

'But there's nowhere to sit,' he complained. I thought, 'Maybe that's better,' but I said, 'No worries, we can keep walking. Do you mind paying, though? I don't like bringing my wallet when I go out.' Caiman ordered a bun, and I ordered three.

'I could eat a horse…' I said, bashfully. And since he didn't mind, I ordered a couple of pies too.

We walked. I took a bite and groaned – my stomach rumbled. And the joy! The relief of that moment: it wasn't egg or tuna, it wasn't beans!

'Thank you so much,' I said to Caiman. He didn't take his eyes off me.

'What do you feel like doing?'

I thought, 'I'm tired.' I said, 'I'm tired.' And then, 'I live nearby.' He wanted to walk me home. I felt obliged to let him.

At the front door I had a brainwave.

'I'm sure we'll meet again, at the club,' I said.

'To be honest, I don't think I'll be back there,' Caiman replied.

'Oh yeah? How come?'

Then he glanced back at the street – down one end, then the other – and said nothing. It pissed me off. Then he lunged in for a kiss.

'No,' I said, clutching my bag of food. I waved goodbye.

But at the window, seeing him from inside, I decided to reward him: I took off my shirt and gave a big stretch, overstating my tiredness, or flaunting it. Caiman looked me up and down, walked towards me. I stood in the middle of the window frame for a long time. Then I went to my dad's room and woke him up.

'Got you a bite to eat,' I said, pleased with myself.

Nights went by. Time passed.

I kept going back to Luna whenever it was free to get in. There was a different show on every night: sometimes you'd find bathtubs dotted about the dancefloor, with men in them, covered in suds and water, inviting us to scrub their backs or jump in with them. Some of the bathtubs were dry: these ones had four marble (or plastic) legs and a young naked man standing in the middle, pretending to be a statue. Crowds gathered around them, and even, occasionally, peed on the men, turning them into a reverse fountain. They moaned and gargled under those warm jets. Then, their golden shower over, they regained their stone-like appearance.

There were underwear nights, too. We'd strip off at the door to spend the whole night dancing in our underwear, brushing past each other…

'Easy now,' Luna would say if she noticed someone stripping completely naked. 'Easy, that's not allowed.'

And Luna didn't make the rules: the club was regularly raided by the police – to keep an eye on things, as they put it. They kept shutting the place down. Sometimes they'd close the doors for weeks on end, ruling that Luna – the place and the person – had violated such-and-such codes.

Since no one ever knew if they'd find Luna open or closed, lots of people stopped going, especially those from other parts of town. Whenever I went there for a dance and came upon shut doors – a full white moon – I just crossed the street and went into The Letcher. At the very least I'd find the Toupées there, at the back, propping up the bar; and often my dad, too, trying to convince them to go in on some scheme or other.

'It's very simple,' I heard him saying to them once. 'Sitting looking out of our window is like looking at art.'

'But I don't get it,' Simón said. 'We have to pay to look at the street?'

'To look at it from *my* window, old fella. Paintings forming before your eyes. Here, let me give you an example: "Still Life with Bins".'

'I'm not buying it, to be honest.'

Luna would come to The Letcher too: she'd sit in

a corner and drink beer after beer, having angry, bitter rants, whether or not anyone was there to listen. She'd rail against the police – 'Those sonsofbitches!' – before downing the bottle and complaining about how much she missed the club shows.

'They're my lifeline,' I'd overhear her saying, or she'd say to me, 'And they're a lifeline to all the regulars. You know that.'

I did know.

Sometimes drunks would sit down beside Luna and tell her about their experiences of the place. Quite a number complained about the hostile crowd (I wasn't keen on it either, especially the rivalry between certain kinds of men, who seemed to police the place while dancing, instead of dancing for fun). Ramón-Ramona would sit and listen to her too.

'Oh, Lunita, I know you're sad, but my bar fills up when your club gets shut down.'

The lockdowns were lasting longer, and the bar district felt more and more desolate. Ramón-Ramona would grow jittery again, and press the customers to drink up.

'You'll never get drunk at that pace! Have one more and I'll give you another half on the house.'

'I look at you and I'm all confused. What exactly are you?' a man asked one night.

'Can't you tell?' Ramón-Ramona asked in return.

'I can't, no. That's why I asked. Are you a man or a woman?' the man went on.

'Come here and I'll show you,' Ramón-Ramona said. A second later, having got a flash of the underside of Ramón-Ramona's apron, the drunk took off with his head hanging down.

Nights went by. Time passed.

We bought on credit, we borrowed. We sometimes

earned a bit of cash, not much, doing odd jobs: baking pies, mending trousers… There was less and less work to do as fewer people were living in the area. Ramón-Ramona helped us out with the odd bit of cash or food, and we'd return the favour by staying at the bar till the end of the night to clean tables and collect bottles… Whenever Luna opened the club – when she was able to, that is, and the police had bigger fish to fry   I went there for a dance.

We started job-hunting again. We knocked on doors: some were opened just a crack and then immediately slammed in our faces; others remained bolted shut. 'There's no money,' people would say to us. 'There's no money.' So we'd trudge back home, my father thinking aloud again, dreaming up extraordinary businesses, extraordinary incomes, while I'd think in silence, wondering what to do: whether to leave my dad all on his own, lost at sea, in order to go and find my own place; or whether to stay for his sake, to look after him while, at the same time, we went on looking for a job for both of us.

'Only me tonight, sorry. You'll just have to sit there and listen to me singing,' Luna joked in front of the crowd one night. 'Can't you see my hot naked dancers have left me hanging?'

The disappointment was audible.

'Ooooh!' 'Nooo!' 'Boo!'

'Just kidding,' Luna shouted back, 'I actually had to sack them cos they couldn't get it up anymore. You buggers milked them dry!'

Glasses clink, laughter.

Other times she spoke what appeared to be the truth.

'We're broke, we can't afford the boys' wages. But I'm going to sing for you. I'm going to give you a lovely, sexy time.' And she'd start: '*I want you far, near, in, out. And you want me far, near, in, out. I love you a lot, a bit, on top, below.*

And you love me a lot, a bit, on top, below…'

At times Luna would burst with passion – with poverty, with love – and wail songs that to her, to him, were sad: '*No, I'll never fall in love again….'*

Nights went by, the massacre happened.

They looked like sculptures, those halved and quartered bodies, impaled on a stake, or displayed inside street lights, raped for the rest of time by a tree. They looked like clay figures, as well. Others, beaten to a pulp, looked like lumps of mud.

The streets became empty, or nearly empty, and it felt darker.

When the police arrived, several nights after the deaths, and they started to collect the bodies - or rather, to toss them into a lorry – some people spoke about handling them with care. 'Don't dump them like that!' they pleaded. 'Don't dump them like that, they can feel.' The police responded with shots into the air, one of which I thought had destroyed my dad's heart. But all that remained of that fright was a scrape on his leg. When the lorry left, when the police left, I asked Pa, contorted by hunger myself, if he wanted something to eat.

'Don't worry, son. We'll eat soon.'

We said the same thing many times – 'We'll eat soon' – on many nights.

'We'll eat soon.'

The club remained closed.

Time passed; time happened, but sometimes nothing else did. I remember lying in bed one night, drenched in sweat, exhausted by the heat, staring at the ceiling and trying to think. I couldn't think – or rather, I can't now remember having thought. The odd flashback, yes. Olguita's funeral – the misted-up glass; the coffin suspended in mid-air; the bin bags soaring on the wind… Time spun on itself: I had visions of us moving to the neighbourhood, of me naked in the red room, on the swing, receiving a thousand men.

On one of those nights, my dad suggested we go down to the sea.

'Maybe it's left us a gift.'

I put on a shirt and my shoes, and we set off. There wasn't anyone out on the streets.

'They should have left them all there,' my dad said as we walked through the bar district.

'Who?' I asked.

'The bodies. They should have left them all there so we'd remember them.'

Suddenly I felt *something*: a combination of tenderness and terror.

We were silent for a while, and then I spoke.

'How could you even think such a thing?'

He didn't reply.

The sea was roaring.

As soon as we set foot on the beach, I told my dad not to take off his shoes.

'Pa, there's broken glass in the sand.'

We watched the waves, waiting for them to bring us gifts. They washed up clocks, all showing different times, and frying pans, stones and something that was either a wig or a hairy scalp.

'It's been a tough few nights,' my dad said, looking up at the sky.

The sofa that had once been red was still there, covered in seaweed, the sofa that had once been a sofa. And inside the hollowed-out seat back, a bird's nest.

Time passed, and continued to pass.

CHAPTER VI

Light

I elongate my eyes with black eyeliner. I stretch them higher too, extending their curve so they reach right up to my eyebrows. Step by step, I back away from myself, checking myself out, admiring myself. My black glittery shirt sparkles in the mirror. I turn around to inspect my back, the skin exposed in places. I inspect my legs. Taking a pair of scissors, I cut my trousers to reveal more of my bare knees and thighs. Before heading out, I touch my chest: the cardboard star is still there, hanging as a reminder of the hard times.

'I'm ready,' I say to my dad, and he appears in the doorway sucking on a bone. He looks at me and pauses for a moment.

'Very good,' he says, but he's not very convincing. 'Something's missing. Something important.'

He dashes out of the bedroom.

'I'll wait in the living room,' I call out to wherever he went.

The table is laden with fruit and biscuits. Rolls and cheese, jam... I eat a piece of pineapple.

'Eat up,' Pa says. 'There's more where that came from.'

He's carrying a dark, shiny plastic butterfly. He comes over to put it on me.

'That's better. Now you're set,' he says, clipping it onto my ear. Then he kisses me on the forehead.

'See you later?' I ask him.

'See you later, darling son. Either at the bar or back here.'

My father sits at the table and slices a watermelon and some garlic bread; he munches on sesame bars. With his mouth full he grabs the remote and switches on the television, which is on mute. He turns up the volume until we hear a man shouting, 'The end of the world is nigh!' I spoil my dad and return his goodbye kiss.

The street outside is lit up. I'm still not used to it.

* * *

One night, on our way to or from the sea, my dad spotted a light.

'Look,' he said, 'What's that?'

'Light,' I replied.

'Well, yes, but where's it coming from?'

We decided to walk towards it. It was coming from high up; from the sky, it seemed.

'What is it?' my dad repeated. 'I don't understand.'

We walked a little closer: it wasn't one light but two, positioned at the very top of some kind of structure. The brightest was pointing down to the ground, bathing a group of sweaty, shirtless men at work mixing cement. The other was illuminating two huge metal girders, infinitely taller than us (and yet, when we tried to see them from the house a few nights later, they were fully engulfed in the darkness).

'Look, son. They're building houses,' my dad said. But no sooner had the words left his mouth than a workman came over to correct him.

'Actually, it's a theme park.'

I jumped up and down with excitement.

'People are going to come back to the neighbourhood,' I said. 'It'll fill up again!'

'There'll be light,' I thought.

Grinning from ear to ear, my dad turned to the workman.

'Hey, pal, I don't suppose you need a hand?'

'Make that four,' I added.

The man looked at us surprised.

'You mean you two?' he asked.

'Who else?' Pa replied. 'We're hard workers.'

The man laughed and turned away.

'Did you hear these lovebirds?' he asked his workmate.

'Don't be stupid,' I shouted back, but even through our annoyance, we were euphoric as we headed home.

And from that night on, we spent our time imagining the changes to come in the neighbourhood.

'The whole place will be lined with street lights,' Pa would say. 'The whole street, right down to the sea. They'll have to do that so the people driving in from further afield can find the theme park without any trouble.'

'They'll all come flocking to the neighbourhood. All the people who left... people who've never even been here before! The Letcher and Luna and all those places will reopen,' I'd say.

And then my dad would take those crowds of people that I was envisioning and put them in places that didn't even exist yet.

'When they've had enough of the Big Dipper, or of bumping into each other on the dodgems, they can come out of the theme park and grab a bite to eat by the sea, in the restaurants that are going to open: fish, vegetables... there's nothing those restaurants won't serve. And for the ones who don't feel like eating, because they feel queasy, say, or because they're already full, well, they can quench their thirst in the bars and cafés that will open all over the place. They'll just pull up a pew, happy as you like, and listen to music, chat, put the world to rights. And we're going to get back to work. You'll see, son. Our luck's about to change.'

With that, my dad would head out onto the pavement and point at the dark street.

'The world doesn't have to be like this,' he'd say.

★ ★ ★

A man is walking another man, who's barking like a dog. Built like an ox, the man-dog is wearing a coppery sequin thong and a leash the same colour wrapped around his neck: the other end of the leash is in his master's hand.

'Good boy,' he says, while the other sniffs around his arse. 'Now fetch.'

The man throws a blue plastic cock into the air, and the man-dog runs after it. The cock falls to the floor, bounces once and lands in a puddle. The man-dog takes it obediently between his teeth and returns it to his owner with a smile. Then he pisses against a lamp post.

I greet them both, blowing them a kiss.

'You look divine,' the man-man calls out to me.

'Woof, woof!' his canine friend concurs.

I give them my blessing with a little nod and carry on, everything around me now an electric forest. Soon enough, I come across three women linking arms, all of them in black miniskirts and with tape covering their nipples: two strips on each one, stuck in a cross shape.

'Lovely evening, ladies' I say.

Next I encounter two hairy topless guys, both in curly wigs, both ridiculously tall and wearing pointy stilettos, impossibly red and high. I can see paper crowns, sweeties, confetti and handcuffs nestling in their wigs.

'Delve in, go on,' one of them says. 'We're wandering lucky dips.'

They laugh. I laugh. Then I bury my hand in the shorter guy's curls and, after groping around for a second, pull out a condom. 'Enjoy!' they say, and then hug me. We walk off in opposite directions.

'Nice to meet you,' someone says to me on the corner of our block. 'I'm Robo-tits.' Her skin is painted electric green and she's moving mechanically, as if her entire body were held together with bolts. She's also wearing a long silver skirt made of plastic, in the shape of an umbrella, and she's holding a fan, which she uses to cool down the people walking past.

'I want to feel,' she says, between long pauses. 'Give me your heart.'

'*Oh, but my darling!*' I reply with one of Luna's songs. '*How am I supposed to love then?*'

Robotits freezes on the spot. She pulls a sad face and then smoke starts coming out of her skirt – dry ice, maybe – as if she's overheating and about to malfunction. All around people are laughing.

'I thought you had no emotions,' one of them says. His skin is painted blue and his beard pink. A drawn-on sea pours from each of his eyes, and from each sea emerges a little boat. 'I want you right here,' he says to me, groping his own arse, and then he disappears, singing at the top of his voice.

A woman is walking her ostrich. She's tied cellophane bows to her hair that are almost bigger than her head. Her pet has the same things on its wings and neck.

'The square's packed,' she says. 'Hurry up!'

I pet the bird and say thanks.

In the square – 'Massacre Square' as it came to be known – a man on a bicycle is handing out flowers.

There are soap bubbles in the air and coloured lights turning the sky from purple to blue, and blue to red, green and yellow. There are speakers attached to the lamp posts: the music, however, still hasn't begun. Ramón-Ramona has hung streamers on the door of The Letcher. In the background, twinkling away, lies Steel City: the Ferris wheel, the Slingshot.

I accept a flower and smell it, happy to be here.

★ ★ ★

Every time we went for a stroll along the shore, my dad and I would stare at the lights over by the construction site. The area they lit up rapidly expanded. The two floodlights at the top of the structure became four, and that same structure began to multiply: two, ten, sixteen shining masts. In just a couple more nights, there were thirty.

Soon you could see the light even at a distance. From the house we'd say, 'They're really making headway,' or, 'They're building faster than we thought.' In the bar, Ramón-Ramona would get excited looking out the window at the landscape awash with new lights. And the same went for Luna, who began to do her own optimistic accounting (or 'living in cloud-cookoo-land', as she would say).

'I'm getting my outfits ready because this shit is about to explode!'

'We have to plan your comeback, sweetie! The grand reopening,' we'd say to her, fully invested in her dream.

'Ohhh yeah,' she'd reply. 'You ain't seen nothing yet.'

We joked around, but we also grew impatient.

'When *are* they going to open the theme park? How much longer?'

Until, finally, Steel City did open its doors. The four

of us went together on the opening night, courtesy of Ramón-Ramona and Luna. To get in we had to go through the mouth of a giant neon cat that was constantly changing colour and expression: in seconds it went from being orange and furious to pink and pensive. The ticket office was inside the mouth (it was one of the cat's teeth), and to get there you had to walk along a red path (its feline tongue).

'My club was way more exciting than this,' Luna can't help saying, the moment we arrive. 'Wasn't it, though?' and she looks at me. 'Wasn't it? It takes more than some cheesy technicolor critter to impress me.'

Once inside, the cat's tongue forks and we have to choose between Love Lane, which would take us to the Ferris wheel, or Avenue of the Abyss, which led to the Big Dipper and the Slingshot.

'They sure aren't making it easy for me,' Luna grumbled, 'I'm not one for love, as you know, but the abyss...'

'This way,' Ramón-Ramona said, pointing to a couple, 'Let's not overthink it, OK? I want to open the bar later.'

Down Love Lane there was a gold and white carousel, shimmering with yellowish lights. Different creatures bobbed up and down as the floor beneath them spun in circles: a silver unicorn, a silver bull and what looked like a man, also silver, on all fours.

'Feast your eyes on that,' Luna said, pointing him out, 'I know which one you want to ride.' Ramón-Ramona seemed to enjoy the joke.

My father was taking it all in silently, as if soaking up the lights, or committing every detail to memory.

'Beautiful, isn't it?' he said to me, and his eyes welled up.

I hugged him, welling up too. Arm in arm, we carried on our way.

There were couples all around us, strolling, kissing, queuing to go on the carousel.

'Like I said,' a man was yelling at his partner. 'This place is a dump.' I looked at him, curious to find out what he was talking about.

'I told you,' the woman snapped back. 'I told you it wasn't worth visiting.'

I was shocked and hurt.

'We came all this way,' the man went on. 'And what did we find? Some fairy lights and balloons.'

My dad, meanwhile, was gazing at the Ferris wheel in amazement. He didn't seem to have heard the couple.

'Come on, it's not that bad,' the woman said, trying to calm the man down. 'Let's just go home, end of story.'

I calmed down too, and spoke to my dad.

'What's caught your eye?' I asked him.

'Everything's spinning.'

The carousel was spinning, and so were the bumper cars and the Ferris wheel. The children were spinning, to get dizzy. The Pirate Ship was spinning around and around before hovering in mid-air, upside down, leaving all its passengers suspended: whole minutes spent with their legs in the air and heads dangling. The Crazy Octopus was spinning too, for the toddlers and the elderly – not as fast as the other rides, of course. And at the far end, on Avenue of the Abyss, the sadistic Slingshot tossed people up into the sky as if they were stones and the moon was a bird.

'What's that horrendous thing?' Luna shouted. 'There's no way I'm getting on that.' We could hear laughter and whooping.

We kept walking and bumped into Yadira selling balloons and candy floss.

'Gotta make a living somehow,' she said, though it wasn't clear whether she was pleased with herself or merely resigned. 'How've you been?'

'Excellent, excellent. Job hunting, you know,' my dad said before any of us could get a word in.

'Look at all the things Olguita is missing out on,' Yadira replied, suddenly morose, and pointing randomly about her.

I could feel my blood begin to boil and I looked away. Ramón-Ramona bought a balloon from her.

'Let's go that way,' Luna suggested, and we took a shortcut to the Avenue of the Abyss. Beside the Scorpion – the roller coaster – was a ramshackle house, either under construction or in ruins. 'House of Horrors,' it said on a sign, and below: 'Coming soon.'

★ ★ ★

'Your old man doesn't come out anymore!' Ramón-Ramona hands me a beer, collects the tips people have been leaving all over the bar, then says: 'I don't know what you bought a TV for. If he's not watching the news, he's watching some soap or cartoon. That's all he does now.'

'He's tired,' I say. 'But he might come out later.'

'Hm. I'll believe that when I see it.'

A young man leans against the bar. He's wearing boots and a flesh-coloured thong, and he's wrapped from his waist to his neck in a feather boa. He tries to speak, but the words won't come. He tries again, then hiccups and covers his mouth with his hands.

'No, sir!' Ramón-Ramona tells him. 'Go vomit somewhere else.'

The man attempts to stand up, but flops back against the bar.

'Same again,' he slurs. 'With plenty of ice.'

Ramón-Ramona pats him on the head and passes him a bucket.

'There you go, honey. If you're going to vomit, do it in there. Don't you dare make a mess.'

Outside, music starts to play. '*The night is so lush! So lush is the night!*' Someone, a man, starts flapping about and shouting, 'Fight, fight!' People get up from their seats to watch.

'See you later,' I say to Ramón-Ramona, and walk back to the square.

There are two moons now: the one higher up is yellow, and covered in empty seas. The other – white and with eyes and long lashes, smiling – proclaims 'Free entry!' on a speech bubble coming from its mouth.

'Sir,' I hear someone say. 'Sir, excuse me.'

The music stops – I hear a cry, 'That's it, butterflies!' – then starts again. '*And one step two. And two steps three. And three and three and three. And one and two and three…*'

'Sir,' and again, 'Sir?'

Are they talking to me? I turn on my heel: two boys are smiling.

'Sorry sir, can you tell us the way to Lights Avenue?'

How old must they be? One of them is naked but for a white rose covering his cock. The other has white roses stuck everywhere but his cock.

'It's that road over there,' I say. 'Where you see the street lights.'

They thank me and head off.

Then, in the distance, between the two moons, I make out people somersaulting in the air, flung into space by the Slingshot.

★ ★ ★

At home one night, my dad was digging around for some spare change.

'I've found enough for two tickets,' he said eventually,

his eyes all lit up. 'We have to choose: the carousel or the Crazy Octopus,' and he was so ecstatic that light seemed to pour from his mouth as he spoke. Pre-empting my response, he went on: 'The faster rides scare me: the Pirate Ship, the Scorpion, the Slingshot…' After a while, when I still hadn't said a word (being too wrapped up in my worry at not having found us jobs), Pa said: 'Don't lose heart. Steel City's only just opened. It'll take time.'

So we went out, but I couldn't help wondering whether my dad was a patient man, or merely deluded.

We walked up the tongue of the fickle cat, who was green and gleeful just then, and later yellow and frightened. At the box office we were informed that ticket prices had gone up.

'That's enough for entry only,' said the clown in the booth. 'Entry but no rides.'

The man, perhaps at the end of his tether after hours spent standing in the cat's tooth in a sweaty purple wig, finally snapped that he didn't have time for our grumbling.

'If you want to go on a ride, you have to pay more.'

I glanced at my dad, who was mesmerised by the park lights.

'Let's make a run for it,' he said with a wink.

He grabbed my hand and dragged me along as he scurried towards the Avenue of the Abyss.

'Come on,' he kept saying. 'Come on.' A few fellas whistled at us; we bumped into some others by mistake. I rolled my eyes and we started running.

'What are you doing, Pa? Didn't you hear, we can't get on any of the rides without tickets.' My dad didn't say a word until we reached the House of Horrors.

'See that?' he asked me. 'That's the place.'

I saw a guy – a belly, a moustache – kicking a piece of wood.

'I have to do everything around here!' he yelled. 'What a mess.'

Slowly, my dad approached him. He gave a little cough before speaking, to avoid startling him.

'Good evening,' Pa said. 'Sorry to bother you, but my son and I are looking for work, and it appears you could do with some help.' The man glanced at him, in irritation and then interest.

'All this is mine,' he said, pointing at the ramshackle house but without taking his eyes off us. He asked what we did and what kind of skills we had, and my dad spoke to him in great detail about Nibbles, our old shop.

'Also, not wanting to blow my own trumpet or anything,' Pa added, 'but I actually developed and managed my own attraction in this very neighbourhood, some time ago now. The Talking House, perhaps you've heard of it.'

I looked at my dad agog, holding in my laughter. The man, on the other hand, was outraged.

'Just a minute now,' he said, 'I'm the only manager around here, and that's the end of it.' I wanted to laugh even harder, but the man went on. 'There's a lot to do before we can open: monsters to make, scary stories to come up with. You'd better get started right away.' He handed us a few banknotes, before adding, 'I want everyone around here to think my name is Danger. You two can call me "Sir".'

I wasn't laughing now so much as rolling my eyes.

Guided by Danger, we entered the house. The walls were black and we could barely see ahead of us. Every time my dad took a step, he seemed to bump into something, until eventually Danger switched on the light.

'Behold, my masterpiece,' he said with unexpected solemnity, and I couldn't tell if he was mocking himself or deadly serious. There were planks of wood and tins of paint dotted about the place. Plastic masks with green warts on their foreheads hung from hooks on the walls, their eyes popping out in terror.

'These won't scare a flea,' Danger said. 'I bought them up in the lights district, at a fancy dress shop. A total rip-off: you can't see a thing from behind the mask and it makes you sweat like a pig. The boys who worked here before got fed up of wearing them. They quit one night and left me high and dry, with a long line of people queuing up for a fright.'

'Don't worry, sir,' I told him. 'That won't happen with us.'

My dad looked at me, baffled, and I realised he hadn't been listening to a word Danger and I had been saying. That tickled me, and I squeezed his hand.

'Let's start by covering that up,' Danger went on, pointing at a hole in the wall and the planks on the floor. He handed us a pair of hammers and some nails, and we set to work.

We spent nights making and covering holes and then opening them up again, all on Danger's instructions.

'I want the customers to be scared from the moment they open the door. Let's make a hole here,' he pointed at the floor, 'so they know right from the word go that they're in peril, that they might trip.'

We opened up a hole – more like a little gap, not very deep – but Danger changed his mind.

'I don't want anyone to actually fall. That could cost me an arm and a leg.'

So we covered it up again, with nails and wood, while Danger went on muttering to himself about the house.

'I want it to be claustrophobic. No one should know what they're supposed to be looking out for, what to be scared of. We'll use the masks as a red herring, so people think that's the kind of horror they can expect here: some silly old rubber faces. And just when they think they know what's coming, boom! We'll jump them from behind. I want them to feel queasy, too: they should feel wobbly, vulnerable. I want the horror to really stay with them.'

Often, as we worked, Danger would recount his nightmares to us, to brainstorm ideas for the house.

'I was in a corridor with low ceilings,' he told us one night, 'and it got narrower the further down it I went. Then the door closed behind me and I had no other choice but to keep walking as fast as I could, just getting more and more scared and out of breath. I noticed a rank smell, of vomit, and I could sense someone drawing near me in that godforsaken place. The louder the footsteps, the more intense the stench of vomit. And I was just beginning to feel woozy when I woke up, soaked in sweat.'

Danger told us to put down our hammers, and in a burst of enthusiasm – which reminded me of my dad raving about The Talking House – he said, 'Let's restructure the whole thing to make it look like the hallway in my dream.'

And so we started over. Danger taught us how to mix cement. I ferried bricks back and forth, and together we built the walls. Having completed our tapering hallway, we then modified the surrounding rooms so that people could explore them if they wanted.

Finally, we opened the House of Horrors, eager to fill our customers with revulsion and dread. Danger worked front of house, sitting on the door to charge the entrance fee: he covered his head with a black plastic bag and poked little holes in it for his eyes and nose. My dad and I hid in different rooms to scare the already scared visitors even more. And all the while, plastic spiders were falling from the ceilings and people were bumping into mutilated mannequins, some of which were wearing the green-warted masks.

Our first customers were a group of six teenagers who couldn't stop laughing. They kicked the mannequins and walked down the hallway without batting an eyelid... None of them, however, entered the rooms.

'Is that it?' they asked at the end. 'What a load of bullshit.'

Danger later told us to howl from inside the rooms.

'You know, to make the experience more intense.' He thought for a while and added, 'Start screaming like you're being killed.'

And then, a memory: the diced red flesh of a man (or several) who'd been out dancing on the night of the massacre.

A couple walked in and I started screaming.

'What are you doing? Why? Leave him alone, sir, leave him alone! He's done nothing to you...' And louder, 'Help, please, help! They've got machetes, they've got guns!' And louder still, 'But why? Why? We never bothered anyone.' And, 'They're trying to kill us! Run, run, they're going to kill us all! Why? Why? Why?'

Then, surprised at myself, I continued screaming, 'Why, you bastards? Why, why? Why?'

My dad, meanwhile, didn't say a word.

★ ★ ★

In the square, the crowd has formed a river that flows into the moon: people enter through the door that both separates and connects the street and the dancefloor, and when they do – as before, as always – the moon is halved. The river flows steadily, albeit slowly. And I'm a part of that river.

Everyone is up on the dancefloor: we, the river, become the sea, then a landslide. '*All together now, let's sing! All together now, let's dance!*' A man smiles at me from a distance. I wave back and dance. He walks over without taking his eyes off me. When he reaches me, he tells me his name.

'I can't hear you,' I say, 'the music's too loud.' So he repeats it, slower this time. I introduce myself, still not having caught his name.

The lights flash on and off – white light to black light, black light to white. It looks like the man speaking to me keeps disappearing and reappearing. He asks if I'm having a good time. He asks what kinds of things I'm into, and about my life. I ask him things in return. He's still smiling.

Every time the lights go out we move in: a little closer each time. I brush his hand, and he takes mine. The lights go on and we look down at our interlaced fingers. The man asks about my butterfly: I tell him about myself, about my dad, my lips right up against his ear. His smile spreads wider.

I draw a little closer during the next flash of darkness, and when the light returns, a few seconds later, I place my lips against his: not yet a kiss. He puts his hands under my shirt, caressing my back, up and down. He opens his mouth, and the kiss ensues. I pull back, look at him: then we kiss and kiss.

We're interrupted by applause, shouts from the crowd. I think, 'It's Luna, Luna's coming out,' but on opening my eyes I see something else. Cages are being lowered from the ceiling – giant, square cages with men inside them. From below, we celebrate their descent.

And then Luna does appear, adorned from head to toe in red sequins.

'Out you come!' she starts calling. 'Come on, out!' And boom, boom, clash, clash! The man I kissed is beside himself with excitement: he hugs me and jumps up and down. He can't take his eyes off those prison cells. 'Come out!' Luna continues. 'Come out!'

Still airborne, the cages begin to open.

'This is beautiful,' the man says. 'Beautiful.' His excitement moves me. The lights go out, then come back on. Everything is light. Boom, boom, clash! Boom, boom, clash! Then suddenly, silence: no more music.

'Fly!' shouts Luna. 'Fly, fly... butterflies!'

* * *

'Leave them alone, please! What have they ever done to you? What have they ever done?'

I kept on screaming in the House of Horrors, every night, as though I were the one being killed. 'Watch out! Help! They've got machetes, guns!' And more, 'Run, run!' And louder, 'No! Leave us alone!'

* * *

The men leap out of the cages and hang in the air, suspended on ropes. Then they spread their arms wide in a synchronised motion, showing off their colourful wings to the crowd – they can inflate in the wind, butterflies: they absorb it, swallow it, and then they grow, their wings swell, becoming up to fifteen times bigger.

'Fly, fly!' Luna goes on, and, seeing the crowd gawping, in awe of the flight, she bellows, 'Keep on dancing, butterflies!'

* * *

We spent our first pay cheque from Danger on a meal out. We put on our glad rags and went to the café which, according to Pa, marked the start of the neighbourhood. They café was called The Fat Shack, and although it was mostly takeaway and delivery, there were a few tables for people to eat at. 'With today's fast-paced lifestyle,' declared a poster in the café , 'there's no need to leave the house: we bring your meal to your door.'

We sat down and asked for the menu.

'We don't have a menu here. Chicken or beans?' the waitress said. We both ordered chicken.

'And if it's not too much trouble, would you mind wiping the table, please? It's sticky.'

The woman turned her back on us.

'Dolores, get over here with the cloth,' she yelled towards the kitchen.

When the cook arrived, covered in sauce and flour, she gave the table a wipe.

'Drink?' the waitress asked.

'We'll have a couple of beers,' my dad said, and the waitress brought us two unopened bottles. She cracked them open and froth came pouring out.

'That's the idea!' shouted Pa. 'That's it, we're celebrating!' She forced a smile and walked off.

We raised our bottles in a toast.

'To you,' I said to my dad.

'To us,' he corrected me, and then, perhaps comparing how carefree we were at that moment to how riddled with anxiety we always used to be, he added, 'and to Olguita and Ramón-Ramona: for their life and friendship. To our work, which will allow us to pay our debts and feel more at peace. To those who lent us money, and to those who turned a blind eye to our existing debt when we had to ask them again. To the end of the hard times. To the light and water we never lacked. To the food which, no matter how late, always appeared on the table. To the health we've been lucky enough to enjoy all this time.'

Listening to my dad speak, I started missing him, right there, even as I sat beside him, devastated by the thought that began to form as he gave his toast: 'This beautiful man is going to die one day,' I thought. And as he continued in his outpouring of emotion, I missed him even more. I said a silent prayer, to try to make myself feel better.

'Be with me always,' I thought, and just then he clinked his bottle with mine.

'Cheers!' he shouted.

'Cheers!'

The waitress arrived with our food.

'The chicken comes with rice and salad,' she said, plonking our plates on the table. The chicken had been slopped all over the rice and was touching – sullying, I thought – the onions in the salad. There was grease on the rims of the plates. We ate every last morsel.

Nights went by and, with the pay cheques that followed, we began to settle what my dad called our 'constrictors': the loans that different companies had given us. 'We'll use my salary to sort out our debts, and yours to live on,' I said to Pa, or he said to me. And so, little by little, we started to pay off what we owed.

We also repopulated the house, or tried to: we recovered the things we'd pawned – a table, some pots – and bought items we wanted or needed: a bed for me, a sofa for the lounge. Sometimes we bought underpants and socks, a shirt, some trousers. A pair of shoes, which we'd take turns wearing: one night I'd wear the old ones and my dad the new ones, and the next night we'd swap.

Further down the line, when the only outstanding debt was the rent, we bought a second-hand TV with a flimsy antenna and weak signal. One evening, as the two of us sat resting in the living room after work, we watched as the news told the story of a man who flew up into the stratosphere in a hot air balloon: he went up, he said, because he wanted to re-enter the planet from above. They showed images – of the sea, the earth – that the man had filmed from incredible distances. Someone asked him what he had enjoyed most about his adventure, and without thinking twice, he replied, 'Being outside the world, if only for a minute or so.'

★ ★ ★

I kiss one. I kiss another. I leave when the butterflies leave. The moon splits in two as I walk out, and, as if in a memory of bygone nights, of old times, the unlit square appears before me: the street lights have been switched off. The darkness has swallowed the signposts. I know The Letcher is still in front of me, even if I can't see it.

A flame bursts into being – a man and his match. The smoke masks the blackness of the fog.

'Shall we get out of here?' the guy asks me. I look at him. He's handsome.

'Let's go,' I say. We don't say a word the whole way.

He lives on the first floor of a building by the sea. In fact, the sea seems to want to touch it, but the waves can't quite reach. Inside, on the inner patio, a group of tenants are smoking. They greet us through the haze. 'Evening,' we say, and go into his flat. The man, I feel, is trying to imitate an actor, or recreate the scene from some movie, because he pushes me onto the sofa and says, smiling, 'I'm gonna give it to you hard.' I try not to laugh, to avoid spoiling the mood; I simply look him in the eye and throw my arms around him, to let him know that I'm relaxed, that I'm into it.

He takes off my shoes, and then my shirt. Then he switches on another light before continuing to undress me. Once he's done that, he resumes his act, crossing his arms and contemplating me calmly, as though I were a landscape or a painting. Maybe I am.

'You look better naked,' he says. I sit up to kiss him

but he pushes me back onto the sofa. He slips a finger inside me, smells it. Then he invites me to bed.

As we enter the bedroom, the first thing I notice are the white pleated drapes, which I presume are covering windows. I look at myself naked. I look at him dressed. I think, 'I like it this way,' but I hear myself ask, 'What about you?'

'I don't do naked,' he says. I grow hard.

He pulls me towards the bed and asks me to kneel down on the mattress. He licks in circles around my closed mouth. Kneeling, afterwards, I try to bring his hand to my cock.

'No,' he says, pulling it away. On the bed I receive his kisses: on my arse, up and down my crack.

'This is what I want,' he says. They become flowers, his kisses. The stars are shining. He doesn't stop licking.

He takes a small bottle from his pocket. And then, a memory: the swing, the labyrinth.

'Do you want some?' he asks. I do. The man draws near, unscrews the cap. We both inhale. More flowers.

I close my eyes, everything feels more intense. And his moans become hands.

The man enters. My legs are propped on his shoulders.

There's no pain, but I offer him expressions of pain, which he receives gleefully. And he says, 'Look at me. Look at me while I fuck you.' I look at him, then: at first I'm irritated, then I feel strong. I turn that strength into sighs and moans, into violent echoes of his voice.

He draws back the curtains and turns me around: below, the tenants are smoking.

'There,' he says, 'so they can see us.' He enters again, fucks me again. 'I like being seen,' he says.

My dazed state turns to joy when I lock eyes with one of the tenants outside. Now I pull faces, change positions. But my lover doesn't want me to move: he takes my hands and pulls them behind my back, where he holds them in his.

Every now and then I scream.

The man stops suddenly.

'I don't think I'll finish tonight,' he says, and he slides out of me. 'Stay over if you like.'

I say no, but thank him. As I step outside I hear applause: it's the tenants giving me an ovation. I wave at them and laugh. I blow them a kiss.

Later, on arriving home, I see my dad has left a note on the table.

'Leaving you this in case you're hungry when you get in.' But there's nothing on the table: no bread or cheese or jam or fruit. No cookies or sesame bars. My dad is fast asleep in his room. Sated, I think, having eaten his fill.

★ ★ ★

With the construction of the theme park, the surrounding areas began to change, just as our house had changed. Food returned to our house, just as light returned to the neighbourhood: it poured from the street lights that had once contained heads. But new street lights were also fitted along the streets. And just as the TV filled our house with all sorts of new scenes and people, the neighbourhood, too, saw the arrival of new things. As my dad said one night, 'When the light came, the scenery was no longer just darkness.' The scenery became scenery.

As people moved in or moved back to the area, as the closed-down shops reopened their doors and new shops and cafés cropped up, the bar district came to be known as Massacre Square. 'There were bodies everywhere,' we heard people say. 'There were severed arms everywhere.' 'They cut off their legs and threw them over there.' Sometimes I wondered whether the people saying such things had actually been out dancing that night. I rarely joined in their conversations.

For a long time, the threat – 'Keep on dancing, butter-flies' – remained scrawled on the wall, in memory of the dead, maybe, or to avoid goading the killers: nobody dared to remove it. One night, though, crossing the square, we noticed the wall had been painted white. Instead of that menacing warning, there was now a plaque that said, 'In memory of us.'

The rest of the city, the electric forest, was steadily filling with the ambulance sirens we heard on TV. Our neighbourhood was no longer the only target, according to the news, and I wondered whether the violence had become more brutal or merely spread. Other TV shows taught us about different discoveries in space: diamond planets; planets with two stars; worlds like Earth, only twenty times bigger.

That's what we did on those nights: we remembered the possibility of violence, while at the same time learning how, beyond our world, millions of light years away, there were places of indescribable beauty.

★ ★ ★

Still tired from all the dancing at the club, still enveloped in the memory of the man's moans and his neighbours' gaze – and their applause – I scream my frightful howls in the House of Horrors. 'But why are you going to kill me? Why? I haven't done anything to you, show some respect!'

I do it against Danger's orders. More than once he's asked me not to keep screaming that stuff.

'A shriek will do. You don't need to reel off full-blown stories.'

My dad uses his role to complain of the hunger he no longer feels.

'Something, at least, anything! A cup of soup, some rice,' he pleads. Our screams cancel each other out.

Towards the end of the shift my throat starts to hurt. I fall silent. Now it's only my dad doing the screaming.

'Can't you see I've got a son? Can't you see? Help me!'

And then, a memory: my dad in a shop pointing at me, begging the owner to let him buy on credit. Hearing him upsets me.

A couple enters the House of Horrors: two boys. They laugh and discuss what they can see.

'I've heard there are rooms,' one of them says, and they come into mine: I don't scream at them but they're scared all the same. I laugh listlessly.

'We're closing soon,' I say.

My dad keeps screaming.

The boys glance at each other and hold hands.

'Stay in here, I'll go,' I say to them. When I reach the door, they hand me a couple of notes. Then they kiss. I leave them to it, and go into the room where my dad is: I tell him to calm down, that no one is listening. His eyes are watery and his skin red. The veins on his neck are popping out like two hearts.

'Easy now, Pa.'

When the boys leave, we tell Danger our shift is over. But instead of letting us go, he takes us to task.

'I couldn't hear you screaming for ages. You still have to scream even when there's no one in there, you know. That's what draws people to the House.'

I tell him that sometimes our voices give out, that we need to stop when our throats start hurting.

'We're not loudspeakers,' I say.

Danger's eyes open wide.

'That's what I need: a microphone and some loudspeakers,' he says, before pausing to consider the idea.

It's good news, I think: if he gets some equipment we won't have to yell so much.

'And a tape recorder, too: we need a microphone, loudspeakers and a tape recorder,' he adds.

I freeze in horror.

'If the screams are recorded, my dad and I will be out of a job,' I think.

'With all due respect, sir, a scream on a loudspeaker feels manufactured,' I say finally, praying Danger will see the value of our craft. We say goodnight.

'Goodnight, yes, goodnight,' he says, distractedly. My dad, I suspect, is oblivious to what that conversation might mean.

'The only scary rides are The Pirate Ship and that thing over there,' a woman says to her friend, pointing at the Slingshot as they walk down the Avenue of the Abyss.

'They toss you up into the air and you spin round and round – just dreadful!'

Her words shake me.

'I'm starting to worry we'll wind up with nothing all over again,' I say to my dad.

'Let's get a bite to eat somewhere instead,' he replies.

The sea roars in the distance.

We stop at a place called The Happy Cow. I order one dish for the two of us to share.

'The portions are huge,' I tell my dad, but he insists on getting one each. The waitress walks away before we can reach an agreement. Then she returns with two plates piled high with rice and topped with greasy warm chicken thighs.

'You see?' Pa says. 'This is better.'

We eat in silence. My dad doesn't take his eyes off his plate. He shovels spoonfuls of rice into his mouth, one after another, and takes tiny nibbles of the chicken, as if to eke it out. When he's done, he lifts his head.

'Let's go to The Letcher and have a beer. I miss Ramón-Ramona.'

We pay up and leave. When we reach the square, my dad says he feels hot. I notice he's walking slowly and think maybe he's tired or full of rice. I think, 'He's getting old'. I pat his back.

At The Letcher, Ramón-Ramona steps out from behind the bar to give my dad a hug and greet him enthusiastically – 'At last you grace us with your presence, dear friend!' – before returning to serve us two beers. The place is pumping, with people chatting and waving their arms in the air, cheering and singing along to the tune. The laughter swells.

'Guess who was just here?' Ramón-Ramona asks us before replying immediately, as if the answer weren't obvious enough: 'The Three Toupées!'

It's as if I could see them yammering away in the corner of the bar. I suddenly miss them.

'And when's that shameless bunch going to come crawling back to the neighbourhood?' my dad asks, chuckling, as he sips his beer.

'They're not interested in moving back to these parts,' Ramón-Ramona says.

A woman overhears us. Furious, or perhaps just drunk, she butts in.

'Who wants them here, anyway? Let them stay wherever they went.'

We order another beer.

'That's what I like to see. Settle in for the night. Who'd choose the TV over me, anyway?' Ramón-Ramona says, strutting and shimmying behind the bar.

My dad laughs and raises his glass. I think, 'He's going to drink a toast,' but instead of speaking, Pa holds his arm in mid-air. Then he opens his mouth, but instead of words, a sound comes out. 'Can he be drunk already?' I think, and just then his arm plummets. The frothy beer sloshes everywhere as his glass slams down on the bar.

'For God's sake,' the woman says. 'Some people just can't hold their drink.'

I leap from my seat the way the beer froth leapt from the glass and I run to him. I can feel a chasm opening up inside me.

'Pa, Pa, what's wrong? Pa!'

Ramón-Ramona rushes to our side.

'What's wrong? Was it the drink? Already?'

My dad slumps down on the bar.

'Talk to me,' I say. He tries to show me his muddled tongue.

Then one side of his face, the right hand side, seems to slide away down his head.

'He's having a seizure,' I start to scream. 'Help me, please, my dad's having a seizure!'

I start shaking, losing my mind. What do I do? What do I do?

'A car! Please! Who has a car?' I yell. Ramón-Ramona turns off the music and calls out, asking who has a car while cupping my dad's face. My dad's eyes start welling up. I hold his hand.

'Pa, squeeze my hand, squeeze my hand.'

He doesn't. I take his other hand: he squeezes feebly. His face is contorted into half a frozen smile.

People are staring at us from their tables: in pity, in shame.

'Has no one got a car?' I ask, hands flailing. At last a man comes over to us.

'Come on, I'll take you,' he says.

We try to pick Pa up, but he keeps slumping to the ground and we can't do it.

'Best to call an ambulance,' Ramón-Ramona says, reaching for the phone. I kiss my dad all over his face.

'You'll be alright, my love, don't worry,' I say.

My dad only stares.

Several customers come and give us advice.

'Don't hold him by the armpits...'

'Let him stay where he is, in that position...'

The woman at the bar downs her drink.

'When the ambulance gets here, don't bother rushing,' she says. 'It won't undo what's happened.'

Meanwhile, Ramón-Ramona insists on asking my dad questions.

'How do you feel? Are you in any pain?'

Silence.

'Can you hear me? Raise a finger if you can hear me.'

My dad raises his thumb.

At last, the ambulance arrives.

'Finally!' I scream at them. 'Finally!'

The paramedics race over without looking at me. There are two: one I've seen before, perhaps at Luna. The other is much younger. Between them they place my dad on a stretcher and, almost effortlessly, they pick him up to take him away.

'There's only space for one in the back,' one of them says.

'I'll go. I'm his son,' and I follow them out holding my dad's hand in mine.

'I'll close up here and meet you at the hospital,' says Ramón-Ramona.

I hear the words but can't think what to reply.

In the ambulance I pray to my dad. I ask him to get better, I tell him he's going to be alright. He lies in the back with his eyes closed: I squeeze his hand, he squeezes mine. When he opens his eyes, he stares at me. And when I lean in to kiss him, his grimace looks even worse. I don't want him to see my shock.

When we get to the hospital – the Medical Centre, as

they call it – the nurses ask me to wait in A&E.

'Nobody tells *me* what to do,' I reply, defiantly, as I wait for them to bring the stretcher out. The nurses look at each other, then they look back at me.

'Sir, you need to calm down,' one of them says.

'You just do your job,' I snap back and then flush with shame. I'm desperate. The second they bring my dad out, I say, 'Bye, Pa. I'll see you very soon.' We begin to cry.

All the seats are taken in A&E. The other people in the waiting room are talking, going over their respective tragedies. They are sayings things like:

'She was stabbed…'

'They found her wounded like that…'

'We've been in here for hours and no word yet.'

I lean against the wall in one corner of the room. A man looks at me. Sensing he wants to start a conversation, I turn away. I refuse to let our pain be a topic for small talk.

How long have I feared this moment? I remember the nights spent lying on my dad's bed, back in the hard times, both of us staring at the ceiling. Or watching him as he slept, listening to him snore, amazed that he was able to sleep despite everything he was going through, and asking myself, 'What will I do when he dies?' incapable of imagining my life without him.

Ramón-Ramona enters, wide-eyed and afraid, and looks around for me, but I don't wave: I simply wait to be found.

'My darling,' Ramón-Ramona says. 'I'm so sorry, sweetheart. What did they say?'

'Nothing,' I reply.

★ ★ ★

'Any news?' I kept asking the doctors that night. The doctors, the nurses, or anyone sitting in reception.

'Nothing.'

I asked for clarification and, in return, the hospital staff asked me for more information.

'Sir, we need your papers.'

'What papers? I don't have any of that with me.'

'You need to bring them so we can admit your dad.'

I lost it and started screaming.

'You haven't even admitted him yet? You fuckers! Fuckers, the lot of you! Bastards! You have to help my dad, you have to!'

Ramón-Ramona tried to intervene, telling me to calm down and that I'd make myself ill.

'Good,' I said. 'What do I care?' And I carried on yelling. Some people in the room began to back me up.

'Have a heart,' they said from their seats. 'Can't you see he's upset?'

Ramón-Ramona took out some money and had a word with a few different employees in the hospital. The staff then decided they would only speak to Ramón-Ramona. They wouldn't even look at me, and if I asked them, 'Anything?', they'd just smile pleasantly and reply, 'Nothing.'

★ ★ ★

A doctor, or someone in a white coat, approaches us, looking over papers and X-rays.

'Are you relatives of the patient?' he asks, solemnly.

We fall all over him with questions.

'How is he? What's the diagnosis?'

When he starts talking, I feel myself emptying out: I hear him say, far away, like an echo, that my dad is in critical condition, waiting for a bed in Intensive Care.

My face drops as the doctor translates what's written on those sheets of paper. I hear the words 'haemorrhage', 'heart', 'a time bomb'... He says Pa can't speak and that the right side of his body is completely paralyzed.

I walk away from him, shut myself off. I picture my dad on the stretcher, unable to speak or move. I start sobbing. And then, a thought comes to me: he's alive, he's in this building. I ask the doctor where he is.

'I want to see him, doctor. He can't stay all on his own.'

Ramón-Ramona cries as well and continues talking with him before coming up to me, I don't know how much later, saying, 'I'm going to get hold of some money. You go with the doctor.'

I follow the man in the white coat. Or rather, I chase after him. I ask if there's any hope.

'I still don't understand what happened,' I say. He explains again, and again I switch off as soon he speaks.

'We'll have to wait a few weeks to see if the outlook changes,' he says.

And I cling to that rock.

We walk into the main hallway of Intensive Care. A row of stretchers spans the entire space, with nurses at each one. The moment the patients see the doctor, they hold out their arms and call to him. Their cries come together in one collective plea. My dad, however, is not part of it: his is a cry that can't be heard.

'Try to hold it together when you see him,' the doctor says to me.

'Mind your own business,' I want to shout, but I know he's right. When I see Pa, a few steps ahead of me, I close my eyes. I'd forgotten the frozen smile.

'He might get better in a few weeks,' I think. And then I approach him, anxiously, timidly. We look at each other, and I smile. I feel calmer now knowing he's calm.

'How do you feel?' I ask.

My dad gives a thumbs up. I kiss his thumb.

'We're waiting for a room for you,' I say, and he starts crying. Did he think we'd be going home? We cry together.

A nurse comes to explain to me that Pa needs nappies.

'He's soiled himself,' he says. 'We need to change him,' and I can't help but feel disgusted.

'I'll go and buy some,' I say, and then, looking at my dad, I add, 'I'll be right back, Pa, wait for me. I'll be right back. You're going to be better in a few weeks. A few weeks, that's all, then everything will be fine.'

'You need to speak into his other ear,' says the nurse. 'He can't hear through that one.'

★ ★ ★

There was a pharmacy on the corner outside the hospital. As I left, I ran into Ramón-Ramona talking to a doctor, although I wasn't sure if it was the same one from earlier or not. As soon as they saw me coming over they went quiet.

'We've got a room for your dad,' said the doctor. Then, looking at Ramón-Ramona, he added, 'It's all taken care of.'

I was glad. I thanked them.

'I'm going for nappies,' I said, in an attempt to seem even vaguely efficient myself.

Ramón-Ramona came with me. They were sold in packs and individually wrapped.

'How many do you want?' the pharmacist asked me.

'If I only buy a few, my dad will only live for a few days,' I thought. So I took out all the money I had on me.

'How many I can get with this?' I asked, handing over almost all the notes.

'Buy nappy cream as well,' said Ramón-Ramona.

'Medium or large nappies?' asked the man behind the counter.

I thought about my dad's belly. I recalled him eating.

'Large,' I said, with a brittle smile. I went back to him with three packs of nappies – twenty in each one – and two tubes of cream.

That purchase calmed me down.

★ ★ ★

The room in Intensive Care is small. My dad lies on the bed with tubes that emerge from bags and then disappear under his skin. There are monitors on either side of the bed: the screens are black; the numbers, white. From time to time, lines and curves appear, sending the numbers up or down. There's a constant beeping sound.

'You lift him up,' the nurse instructs me, 'and I'll clean him.' On the count of three I lift my dad's legs, struggling to hold them up, while she washes him with wet wipes.

'Careful,' she says to me, 'careful not to disconnect the I.V.'

The smell of piss and shit is overwhelming.

'I'm not allowed to feel disgusted,' I think, and I'm horrified to realise that those were the exact same words I said to myself when I had to carry Olguita's body. I close my eyes; the comparison is unthinkable. My dad is alive. My dad is alive. My dad is alive.

'Good,' the nurse smiles. 'Spick and span. Now we need to tidy up the bed. With this lever you bring up the back rest, and this other one does the feet.' When I start to move the first lever, the nurse turns back to my dad.

'Raise one finger when you feel comfortable,' she says. Little by little, I move him into the right position. My dad smiles and gives a thumbs up.

'What a good patient you are,' says the nurse.

To cheer him up, I kiss him on his crooked grin.

'It'll all be OK again in a few weeks,' I repeat to myself.

Soon after, a doctor comes in holding several folders. He greets us matter-of-factly, and checks the numbers on the monitors.

'He's in a very delicate condition,' he says, and I go to pieces. 'We can't touch him.' He begins to list the problems: he talks about his brain, his heart. He talks about medication that will end up killing him. My dad closes his eyes. Ramón-Ramona comes over to coddle him.

'My dad can't speak but he can hear. Have some respect, don't be so stupid,' I shout at him. The doctor, strangely embarrassed and affected, and without taking his eyes off me, changes his tune.

'We need to wait a few weeks. The picture might have improved by then.'

He goes towards the door but stops and comes back.

'You two aren't allowed to stay here,' he says to Ramón-Ramona. I'm falling apart. I lose all hope.

'But how can we possibly leave him?' I plead with the doctor. 'I won't be any trouble, let me stay here with him.' The numbers go down, then up again. The lines become curves, the curves curl tighter. Another doctor pops his head in to ask us to leave.

'Your dad needs some rest.'

'Should I say goodbye?' I think. 'No.'

And then, aloud, I say to my dad:

'See you soon, Pa. Try to get some sleep.'

★ ★ ★

The following night they moved my dad from Intensive Care.

'He's doing well,' a female doctor said to me. 'He's stable. I think we'll be able to discharge him tomorrow.' I was elated. I felt like someone had reached out and stroked me. Afterwards, she explained that they were going to put him in a general ward room.

'He doesn't need such close observation now,' was her parting comment.

I thanked her.

As I waited for the stretcher carrying my dad to arrive, I pleaded with him in my head. I thanked him for having got better, and begged him to go on getting better. I wanted Ramón-Ramona to come. I wanted to share the good news.

Three nurses appeared at the end of the hallway: the one in front was wheeling the stretcher. The other two were holding the drip and monitors. As they got nearer, I recognised my dad: he was asleep with an oxygen mask covering his mouth. Downhearted, or rather, terrified, I ask:

'What have you put that on him for? The doctor told me he was OK.'

The nurses exchanged glances.

There was silence before one of them explained.

'There's no room in Intensive Care. But don't worry, we'll keep a close eye on him here.'

* * *

'I don't understand,' I say to the nurses. 'I was told he was doing better.'

'No, sir. The patient is still in a delicate condition.'

'But that's not what they just told me.'

'That's the information we have.'

Two of the nurses leave, and the other stays to give me some instructions.

'These little numbers here tell us how he's breathing and how his heart is. This number can't go below ninety. And this one, no lower than seventy. If either of them go lower than that, this light will go on, and you'll hear a little beep. If that happens, you call us.'

I stand there staring at her, dumbfounded.

'But where are you going?'

'We'll be right here, on call and on this floor.'

They leave me alone with my dad, who's sleeping with the mask on: you can't see his face. I stroke his cheeks, his hands. One of the monitors reads ninety. The other, seventy-two. Everything's under control.

My mind turns to money. How much is all this going to cost? How much did Ramón-Ramona hand over? I sit on the floor, bone-tired, exhausted from being on my feet. I can look after my dad from down here.

★ ★ ★

The alarm sounded. I woke up. And the red light, the red light: beep, beep, beep, beep, beep, beep.

'What's happening? What's happening?'

And then I remembered the monitors. One read ninety; the other, sixty-two. 'Nurse!' I shouted. 'Nurse!'

I opened the door and shouted louder.

'Help, nurse! Nurse! Hurry! It's my dad!'

★ ★ ★

Four of them appear at the end of the corridor, running. When they reach us I throw myself at Pa, who's opened his eyes, perhaps because of the alarm, perhaps because of my shouting.

'How are you, my love? I'm right here, can you see me?'

Beep, beep, beep, beep, beep. It occurs to me that this is the first time he's seen the new room.

'We've left Intensive Care,' I tell him.

The nurses switch off the alarm and inspect the monitor. 'Seventy-four,' one of them says. The others look daggers at me.

'It went below seventy,' I say, indifferent to their exasperation.

They take my dad's blood pressure and check the tubes and drip.

'Sir,' another nurse chides me. 'You can't scream the place down like that. Can't you see you've startled the other patients? You've startled your own father.'

'I'm sorry, nurse,' I say, 'but the light went on. It was beeping.'

'That beep will sound on and off all through the night.'

* * *

It did keep sounding, and the light kept flashing. Beep, beep, beep, beep, beep: the reminder that Pa was dying. There came a point when the nurses decided to show me how to deactivate the alarm.

'You just have to press this little button here. You know, so we don't have to keep coming in each time.'

I asked them why it went off so often. I asked them to tell me why there wasn't a doctor looking after my dad, keeping an eye on the monitors.

'Those numbers are part of a picture we already know. The alarm goes off because it's sensitive, but nothing's happening that we're not already aware of. His condition is stable.'

From then on, every time the alarm went off, every time the light went on and made the room glow red, I got up to turn it off, more irritated by the sound than concerned about my dad. His condition was stable.

After a while, Ramón-Ramona appeared at the door.

'Why did they move him from Intensive Care? And the mask? No, no, no, no: he can't stay here.'

Beep, beep, beep, beep, beep...

'What happened? Why's he in here?'

I told Ramón-Ramona that his condition was stable, that tomorrow they'd be able to discharge him.

'And the mask? No, no, no: your dad is very ill.'

My friend left the room to look for a doctor.

Beep, beep, beep, beep, beep...

I could make out the shouting.

'I paid you to keep him in there! And the moment my back's turned, you move him, you absolute bastards!'

One of the doctors spoke to Ramón-Ramona and pointed at me. He said things I didn't understand. Ramón-Ramona interrupted him.

'He's not in his right mind. He doesn't realise how ill he is.'

★ ★ ★

I close the door, absolutely crushed, and walk over to my dad. His eyes are closed. I place my hand in his left hand – the one that still has feeling. My dad grips it meekly.

I kiss him and whisper 'I love you' in his ear.

'I love you, I love you.'

He opens his eyes. I'm not sure if I woke him up or if he just wants to look at me.

'Do you know who I am?'

My father's eyes open wider. Ramón-Ramona tells me off.

'What a thing to ask. You're scaring him! He knows what's going on!'

I rest my head on his belly, which rises and falls rapidly.

Doctors come in; nurses come in. They ask me to move so they can wheel away the stretcher. We look at one another again, my dad and I, and then someone speaks.

'We're taking him back to Intensive Care.'

I walk with them, my hand resting on Pa's arm. Our eyes meet for a moment. Someone says to me, 'Sir, you can't come in here.'

A feeling of pain and relief.

Once again, I place my hand in my dad's hand, and leave it there for as long as I can.

We hold each other's gaze.

★ ★ ★

Hours later, a doctor emerged. He was looking for someone – his eyes were searching – and I thought suddenly that it must be me. With slow steps I approached the man, who was standing on tiptoe, craning his neck. When our eyes met he stopped looking. He smiled. I could sense pity. I staggered towards Ramón-Ramona, screaming.

'I know what he's going to say!'

★ ★ ★

I can see myself on my feet holding the three packs of nappies: only one is open.

'Be strong, be strong,' people are saying. I've no idea who they are.

Ramón-Ramona arrives with water and some pills and asks me to take one. We sign forms, make calls.

'Burial or cremation?' Ramón-Ramona asks.

I reply.

'Mahogany or oak?' Ramón-Ramona asks.

I reply.

'We'll have to choose an outfit,' Ramón-Ramona says.

I hear myself reply.

'Lend me some money to buy flowers.'

★ ★ ★

Luna and the Toupées came to the funeral. Neighbours I'd never spoken to before came. They hugged and consoled me. They said, 'I'm so sorry,' and 'My condolences.' When I couldn't muster a smile, I just thanked them.

Yadira also turned up with a bunch of the balloons she sold.

'Do me a favour, sweetheart,' she said. 'Put this over there with your dad.' And she handed me a helium heart. I thanked her. I cried. I tied the balloon to the coffin lid. 'I don't want to see him like that,' she added.

But I did see him like that. I spent the whole time looking at him, speaking to him, draped over the glass.

'He looks beautiful, beautiful,' I thought with relief and gratitude.

Not long before they came to carry him away, I heard someone saying, 'Get him off there. He's torturing himself.' Ramón-Ramona scooped me up in a hug.

'You have to say goodbye now.'

★ ★ ★

An invisible hand, bigger than me, pins me down on the bed: I want to eat and I don't want to. I want to go out and I don't want to. I spend night after night on my back. If I forget that he's dead, I force myself to remember that he's dead.

Sometimes Luna and Ramón-Ramona come by. If I open the door, they stay with me for a while. If I don't, they post money through the door, which I pick up from the floor several nights later.

When I'm truly ravenous I leave the house, only to be surrounded on the streets by people laughing.

* * *

Last night I dreamt my dad was alive.

We were by the sea, both of us sitting on the sand, watching the empty waves. 'Beautiful, eh?' my dad said.

That was the whole dream.

I'm still in bed, his bed, thinking about the last few nights. I think about my dad – everything is my dad – who is even more here since he stopped being here. No, that's not true: my dad was more here when he was here.

His ashes are on the table next to some fruit and a couple of bread rolls. Every time I walk past, I kiss the wooden urn that holds him.

In the living room, his drawings greet me.

* * *

I spend my life asleep so I can be with him in my dreams. Sometimes I wake up with the cardboard star in my mouth. And I leave it in there until I shift into a different position.

I'm overcome with joy one night when I remember the tape recorder. My dad's voice is there inside. I look for it and find it, but can't bring myself to press play. I leave it on the table, next to him. I go back to sleep.

* * *

If I'm not in bed, I'm on the sofa. If I'm on the sofa, I watch TV. A woman is telling another woman to go out and have some fun, to stop being so wrapped up in her own thoughts.

I listen to the woman on the screen as if she were talking to me, and decide to heed her advice. So I leave the house, walking slowly, I cross the square and continue down the streets until I reach Steel City. I buy a ticket for the Slingshot: two seats inside an open sphere; two bungee ropes connecting the sphere to two huge masts on either side.

'Don't you want to wait for someone to go on with you?' the man asks me.

I tell him no.

'Sure you feel safe?'

People begin to crowd around.

'Oh, how terrifying,' they say. 'Terrifying!'

'I'm ready,' I tell the man, and hold on tightly to the safety bar. The seats tilt back. My feet are now dangling in the air.

'Count to ten,' the man tells me, and the crowd shouts in unison, 'One... two... !'

They release me.

I'm not a rocket; I'm a suicide in reverse. I spin in the air. The sea is the sky and the sky is down below. The sea is above, threatening to come pouring on top of me.

I plunge. A void. I plunge into a world where he no longer is. The crowd claps and cheers – 'Well done, lad!' – and I shoot back up to the sea, spinning, and back down to the city, just me, alone in the air. And then something – *something* – in the sky: a light, a flash of colour. The night, golden and sad, coming to an end.

Io adoro le stelle e la notte, ma tu sei il canto del mio mattino.
Alda Merini

In memory of

**GIUSEPPE CAPUTO
CASTIGLIONE**
beloved father and friend

19 March 1942 – 10 February 2015

CHARCO PRESS

Director & Editor: Carolina Orloff
Director: Samuel McDowell

www.charcopress.com

An Orphan World was published on
80gsm Munken Premium Cream paper.

The text was designed using Bembo 11.5 and ITC Galliard Pro.

Printed in July 2019 by TJ International
Padstow, Cornwall, PL28 8RW using responsibly sourced paper
and environmentally-friendly adhesive.

MIX
Paper from
responsible sources
FSC® C013056